Tales of TITANS

From Rome to the Renaissance VOL. I

RICH DiSILVIO

Published by DV Books, an imprint of Digital Vista, Inc.

Cover art by © Rich DiSilvio.

Cover photos of historical figures public domain. Photo of Vespasian by Shakko, photo of Titus by Filipo, photo of Titus Arch by Rabax63, close up by Dnalor 0. Photo of Augustus full statue by Till Niermann. Photo of Columbus and illustrations of Da Vinci's La Rocca Fortress by Rich DiSilvio.

Author's Website: www.richdisilvio.com

- - - - - - - - - - - - - - - - - -

Names: DiSilvio, Rich

Title: Tales of Titans: From Rome to the Renaissance Vol. I / Rich DiSilvio

Description: New York, USA: DV Books, an imprint of Digital Vista, inc.

Identifiers: ISBN 978-0-9976807-8-2 (paperback) |
ISBN 978-0-9976807-9-9 (eBook)

Subjects: Emperors--Rome | Kings, Queens, Rulers | Arts--Renaissance--Italy | America--Discovery and Exploration--Spanish | Historical Fiction--History and Criticism

Illustrations/Photos: 20

CONTENTS

AUGUSTUS: *The Philosophy of Rule*

The life-giving gas rapidly expanded his tiny virgin lungs, following a brisk slap on the back. Thus was Gaius Octavius's first breath of life free from the womb. He would soon learn that it would be an endless struggle to maintain this precious gift, and that even though every breath one takes is by one's own effort, a supportive slap on the back is crucial to survival.

Now in his twilight years, the great ruler, who had come to be called Augustus, or most exalted as the name implies, was reflecting upon his long and illustrious career, with a concerned eye toward the future.

His early rise to power was marked by many near-death engagements on the battlefield, as well as in the perfidious political arena. Quite miraculously, those conflicts had been waged when he was only a mere teenager. Having outwitted perhaps the most learned sage of his age, Marcus Cicero, and beaten the most feared general, Marc Antony, Augustus—a solitary country boy who stepped out of obscurity to seize the greatest empire of his day—had shocked all.

With the lifelong aid of his most trusted general and loyal childhood friend, Agrippa, he had secured many years of peace, which he could now calmly reflect upon and cherish with a ripened grin. Priding himself on his earthy good sense, disdain for the ostentatious, and a paternal persona that would guide and elevate an entire empire, Augustus established what he believed was the only solution to a corrupt and war-ridden Rome. His decisions proved right: he presided over a renewed golden age for over four long decades and had made Rome the wonder of the world. Augustus had much to be proud of.

Inside his modest and unassuming residence, nestled on Palatine Hill, Augustus sat statuesque and pensive on a simple wooden bench wearing a plain toga, looking more like a plebeian than the *Princeps*. Several feet to his left, his wife Livia stood brushing her thick gray hair. She, too, was quiet, yet for a different reason.

The seventy-six-year-old ruler was ill and facing his last months on Earth, and the monumental quandary of choosing a successor weighed upon him heavily. With three bloodline heirs prematurely dead, Augustus had been forced to adopt Livia's austere son, Tiberius, from her former *matrimonium*. Meanwhile, Livia was a strong and manipulative mother who wanted very much to see her son take the reins. However, knowing that her husband was not one to be easily swayed, Livia remained tactfully calm as she went about her daily activities.

Augustus had been gazing at Livia out of the corner of his eye, when he lifted his head. "Livia, with the dreadful chain of misfortune that has besieged me, your beloved son is now well seated to acquire my title. But you must know that I still have serious reservations."

Livia turned and smiled diplomatically. "Augustus, my dear, I have seen you on your deathbed far too many times and you have always managed to miraculously defy the gods. Why do you think those stories of your divine birth spread so quickly? Romans know of no man stricken as often as you or as strong-willed and brilliant as you. You're a unique gift to Rome and your time of passing has not yet come. So, other options may still arise."

Augustus frowned. "I know good fortune has shone upon me many times in the past, Livia, but I've played this role well beyond anyone's expectations, especially my own, and the final act approaches." Augustus peered gravely at the two theater masks painted on the wall. Looking back at Livia, he continued, "My appointment by my great-uncle Julius was not made in haste or from lack of choice. My decision is likewise crucial. Believe me, I am pleased that Tiberius is a competent general, but I can never forget how he abandoned us, as well as the Senate, by fleeing to Rhodes. It was inexcusable. That I allowed his return speaks as much of my forgiveness as it does of my back being pinned against a wall. No leader should find himself ensnared in such a position. And so, I anxiously await the divine guidance of the Sun. Apollo must shed light on this final and most vital decision—he must!"

Livia turned slowly and gently picked up a golden talisman; it was a gift from Tiberius, who had received the reward for his massive triumph in Pannonia. With a loving smile, Livia proudly turned toward her pale husband. "You worry in vain, my dear. Sometimes you afford superstition too much muscle, whether relying upon a piece of sealskin for good luck or the great Apollo for guidance. I trust your good judgment and so should you; it has never failed you. Granted, you may have wanted Marcellus, Gaius, or Lucius to be your successor, but, as you know, unforeseen events are a part of life. Perhaps their tragic deaths were for a reason. You know I loved and raised Gaius and Lucius as my own sons, but you are far too wise not to have noticed their inexperience or ingratitude. Tiberius may have run away to Rhodes, but perhaps that was to allow his younger relatives unhindered access to your title."

Augustus' right brow pinched as he shook his head. "Livia, I do not need or expect Tiberius to think for *me!* I was grooming those boys, who came from the loins of my daughter and best friend, Agrippa. So whatever decisions I made, Tiberius should have simply obeyed. As it was, his foolish retreat has only shed doubt upon his own abilities and *mine* for choosing such a capricious young man."

Livia irritably slammed the talisman down. "Capricious!? You mean the young man who defeated countless armies that could have wreaked havoc all across Rome? Furthermore, that young man is now in his fifties! You were in your teens when *you* sought power."

Augustus grinned. "My dear, being a great general or simply great in years does not necessarily make a great politician. My great-uncle Julius and my feeble, former *triumvir* Lepidus are both proof of that."

Sensing the weight of his words and the sensitivity of the topic, Livia took a deep breath and calmly resumed brushing her hair. "That's true, however, Tiberius has shown great promise, and if chosen, I know he will honor your memory. You shall indeed be hailed as Rome's first and most glorious *imperator*."

Augustus frowned. "You know I dislike that title, Livia!"

"Oh, yes, how could I forget, *Princeps*, or first among equals, is your preferred title. But we both know our fellow Romans all hail you as *Augustus* Caesar. Your deification is assured, and rightly so."

Augustus shook his weary head. "You miss the point. The public does not want to be told to whom they must bow or to idolize. A delicate matter, such as this, takes poise and restraint, as well as genuine talent. Control and respect cannot be won by arrogantly dictating one's own divinity. This I know all too well. Look how Romans still adore the great Cincinnatus. When Rome was under siege, they beckoned him out of retirement and appointed him dictator to secure Rome from conquest. He left his plow and fought a winning campaign for the Republic, only to magnanimously decline leadership in its aftermath." As Augustus continued passionately, he clenched his fist, "He had Rome in the palm of his hand, and could have ruled like a god, but *no*, he gave Rome back to the people. I have always acted as a fellow citizen of Rome. Yes, *the first citizen*, but a citizen nonetheless. Upon my death, my successor may carry out deification if he wishes, but what remains most important, my dear Livia, is what's best for Rome!"

Livia's stiff posture softened slightly as she rubbed her forehead. Pivoting about, she purposefully walked toward him and placed a basket of fruit by his side. With a firm hand planted on her hip, Livia looked squarely into his eyes. "I don't see how that makes a difference. Ramses and many other great pharaohs ruled with iron fists, and the people labored hard and prayed to their greatness, didn't they?"

Nonchalantly, Augustus picked up a cluster of grapes and began freeing them from the vine. Noticing his great grandchildren in the next room, he began tossing the grapes into a nearby bowl, as he replied serenely, "Yes, control they had, Livia, but it was total enslavement, smoldering with resentment. Look what became of Egypt—their laws, language, and culture have all but completely vanished. We may work our plebeians almost as hard, but their minds very seldom abandon hope. Shackling an entire populace is suicide for the public and the state. That explains why the lure of Roman citizenship, legal rights, and a civic duty for religious ritual play such crucial roles in appeasing the masses. The reckless and decadent behavior that destroyed our Republic must always serve as a warning. Roman law must prevail, as excessive freedom promotes mischief and moral decay. Furthermore, it is imperative that we share this ideal of hope and prosperity with all our new provinces, regardless of their distance from Rome. This, my dear, is paramount."

With a clatter of little feet, three of their great grandchildren ran by, each grabbing a handful of loose grapes from the bowl. Merrily, they ran off to the sunny courtyard and began handing some of the grapes out to their begging friends. Augustus smiled, and then looked down at the remaining cluster of grapes in his hand.

He raised them up, and looked at Livia. "You see, my dear, these grapes are still shackled and are destined to my sole wants and whims. I can eat them for nourishment or even wastefully destroy them. However, those that I freed have traveled beyond the walls of this room and managed to nourish and benefit many others. Likewise, we Romans need to travel to other lands and spread this wealth and nourishment."

Livia smiled and nodded admiringly. "Yes, I see your point. But how much freedom did those grapes truly have? *You* freed the grapes and then purposely tossed them in the bowl. So, weren't *you* the silent orchestrator of their destiny?"

Augustus smiled. "Now you are finally seeing the beauty of using power wisely. The minds of the masses must be carefully and subtly conditioned. They must be able to believe that they are free and part of a greater whole, and that there is some ray of sunshine to brighten their days. Why do you think I engage Romans in many grand tasks? It's to remain productive for Rome, for themselves, and to prevent the grapes from rotting on the vine. However, unlike the pharaohs, I shall not humiliate them by demanding harsh labor to construct useless edifices for my own personal glory. Our glorious building projects may serve my personal agenda, but that agenda is for the benefit of Rome and its citizens. No other regime in history has bequeathed to the plebeians the public works we Romans have. Moreover, these great works shall rival and surpass all before us. And between the policies I've created and those of the Republic that I've left in place, Rome will prevail."

Livia turned, and as her eye caught the dark shadow of the sundial in the courtyard, she scoffed pessimistically, "Yes, but the almighty Sun over Egypt has long since set; it has abandoned Egypt's noble attempts at greatness and its people, as it will one day Rome."

Despite his crippling ill health, Augustus rose steadily to his feet and declared firmly, "Never! Providence has always watched over Rome. Even our great poet, Virgil, elucidated this fact." As Augustus continued passionately, his arms reached radiantly outward. "Our grand systems of roads are spreading over distant lands like a sprawling laurel tree, and as it continues to sprout healthy new branches, keep in mind, Livia, that Rome remains its royal root. What were once barbaric lands are now civilized provinces—learning and benefiting from our laws, customs, and grand feats of engineering. Egypt's glamorous eyes only saw Egypt, and blindly neglected the world around her. The grand pyramids may have been magnificent, they may have touched the sky, and they certainly consumed a nation's time and resources, but they only housed one small selfish and shriveling man, a man who callously neglected the needs of an entire nation so that he alone could be glorified."

As Livia stood mute like a lectured pupil, with eyes wide, Augustus pointed out the window at the majestic city, and continued, "My intention, Livia, has always been to bring the glories of Rome to the rest of the world, by building grand forums, temples, aqueducts, and markets wherever we traveled. Moreover, my creation of the *Vigiles Urbani* to apprehend criminals and fight fires in our cities has finally brought order and safety to the chaos that has plagued mankind since its very inception. Those gifts I bequeathed to all of our citizens, and it is the duty of all my successors to ensure the same for all future citizens of Rome. It is our destiny!" Taking a deep breath, Augustus expelled his last charge, "Therefore, Egypt's blind ambition is something I, as a Roman, never understood, could never embrace, and shall never forget! And if my successors fail to fulfill my vision, Livia, it is not because of any so-called cataracts I may have, but rather their own blindness. Therefore, I pray to the gods, my dear, that your son will not only have the bravado to repel foes, but also the brains to see clearly! Rome's future, nay, our civilization's very future, depends on it."

Through instinct and observation, Augustus knew his new empire needed a new frame of mind, as well as initiatives not employed by the Egyptians or any previous regime. Augustus was not what we today would call a well-groomed intellect, however, his innate common sense, extremely organized and analytical mind, along with the ability to learn from his and others' mistakes, made his efforts and achievements beyond brilliant. During Augustus' careful and precarious rise to ultimate power, he had wisely left the Senate and Republican infrastructure intact, albeit with some clever revisions. These policies all had clear objectives.

First, Augustus understood the deep political roots and social-economic pedigree of wealthy patricians. They had held and maintained their positions of power for many decades, with some senators like Brutus having family trees extending back 500 years to the founding of the Republic itself. As such, they and their entrenched network would not easily relinquish power. Caesar had arrogantly underestimated them and it proved fatal.

Henceforth, Augustus needed to purge the Senate of those who plotted against his adoptive father; those who remained needed to be cajoled and placated, which could not be achieved by arm-twisting or arrogantly stripping them of power. Furthermore, the Roman citizens of the day had had enough of civil strife. Over the previous two decades they had been dizzied by having to take sides with one potential usurper after another. Loyalties were strained and national enthusiasm drained. Therefore, it was prudent of Augustus to leave the Senate, and its web of influence, intact to some degree.

Second, Augustus understood that more than one person with a handful of cohorts was needed to run a sprawling empire. The bureaucratic infrastructure that worked so well for the Republic would serve him well too, as long as he made continual subtle revisions that would wrest the ultimate and abused power from the aristocracy.

Third, and quite ingeniously, Augustus realized the importance of creating a new cultural identity for his government that he could share with all the Roman provinces. In an act of perceptive statesmanship and benevolence, Augustus bequeathed what was available in the illustrious capital city to the distant provinces. This extensive policy had many cultivating facets.

To Augustus, it meant that all newly acquired provinces would be outfitted with the utilitarian effectiveness and the grandness that Rome itself enjoyed—this would be an integral part of the glue binding a sprawling and diverse populace. Grand forums, public markets, housing with running water, public baths with spectacular saunas, and other cutting edge facilities not only improved the standard of living, but equally important, it elicited pride of community and Roman culture.

This psychologically effective technique was not lost on subsequent leaders, even those well beyond Rome, and would influence many European nations and America in the distant future. Not only did the American founding fathers emulate Roman architecture and city planning, but even today, the construction of shopping malls and familiar franchises sprawling across America is unifying the nation, visually and psychologically. There is a downside to this trend—namely, the decline of uniqueness—but the mission of spreading unity, national identity, and different forms of progress is achieved.

Needless to say, America's founding fathers scrutinized and utilized many facets of Augustus' political, economic and engineering initiatives, thus validating the immense indebtedness Americans and most other Western nations today have for ancient Rome, and in particular for Augustus.

Moreover, the titanic skills required for achieving all those amazing goals, especially considering that Augustus' provincial education was cut short, thus necessitating a need to devour knowledge, as well as discern the virtues and treachery of human nature, whereby he could act decisively and judiciously, remain to this day immeasurably off the charts.

This new breed of leader, which as Suetonius proclaimed "held idealism over egotism in a noble effort to create the best possible government" had not only made a monumental beginning for Rome, but more importantly, one of seismic proportions for Western civilization. Augustus had only been a teenager when he began his grand and noble quest, yet he prevailed against tremendous odds, and created an amazing enterprise that would profoundly imprint itself upon all future generations. This young man, born Gaius Octavius, and later exalted as Augustus, has been justifiably called "The Father of Western Civilization."

VESPASIAN & TITUS:
Defenders of Political and Religious Integrity

A rancid cloud of war-dust entered the nostrils of Lieutenant Dalius—inciting an involuntary gag. With a violent bark, a murky glob of phlegm jettisoned out of his mouth and viscously cemented itself to the ground. Looking down, he saw the slimy blob begin to congeal with the blood-drenched soil.

Dead carcasses lay strewn about him in every direction as he pulled out a swatch of cloth to wipe his soiled lips. Several yards away, squadrons of cavalry and foot soldiers clashed in the midday plume of death. It was a massive and brutal campaign waged by his commander-in-chief, Vespasian, who was now standing at his side in the Judean province, and would soon be Imperator of Rome.

As the battle raged on, rupturing both flanks, Vespasian turned toward Dalius. "Take heed, I will be taking leave to set sail for Alexandria. Send a message to my son Titus—he will execute the final blow and end this revolt once and for all!"

Wiping his bloody gladius clean, Dalius dutifully nodded. "Yes, Commander, it shall be done."

As Vespasian looked at Dalius' gladius, he retorted in his typical ribald fashion, "Indeed it shall, it's imperative that both Titus and the Jews receive their message… thunderously loud and painfully clear. These rebels are like a burning hemorrhoid, and Titus shall be my gladius to carve these bloody bastards out!"

As Dalius gruffly chuckled, Vespasian added, "There's only so much pain we Romans can take up the ass, after all, we're not Greeks!"

Dalius burst out laughing, as Vespasian commanded, "Now go! We both have our missions to complete."

SEVERAL MONTHS LATER: After subduing the core faction of Jewish rebels, Vespasian secured the seat of emperor by eliminating his three rivals for the throne, which had been left vacant by the suicidal death of Nero. Yet his son, Titus, was still hunting down the last remnants of rebels in the inhospitable Judean province.

Gusty winds screamed through the chiseled chasms as Roman soldiers scurried about with cloths wrapped around their noses and mouths. Despite spending several long months in the Masada Valley, Titus and the 10th legion were far from idle. Their mission had taken them into a barren wasteland where only one edifice stood.

Masada was a fortress that sat atop an enormous plateau, which sharply jutted upward out of the valley's rocky floor. Like a towering Valhalla, Masada was an intimidating structure. Just the sight of it made some soldiers faint of heart. In fact, many soldiers had seriously questioned the probability of ever scaling the huge monolith. However, due to their commander's ingenuity, determination, and patience, their long arduous task was finally complete.

The soldiers had been ordered to build a gargantuan ramp of beaten stone and earth that actually rose up from the valley floor right up to the plateau's summit. Two nights previously, the Romans had fashioned battering rams and built huge structures of interlocking timber, filled with earth, near the fortress' walls. The Romans then rammed the walls, creating large fissures, but the trapped rebels quickly repaired them. In an attempt to smoke out the enemy, Titus' leading commander, Flavius Silva, had ordered the timber to be lit on fire. A billow of thick black smoke at first headed towards the Romans until a providential wind hurled it back toward the fortress. This sign of divine intervention had further strengthened the Romans' resolve.

However, the shock and awe of flames and smoke had died out over the cold night, and the ramp needed mending before sun up. The dawn was now beginning to illuminate the barren valley with golden tones. Meanwhile, pitched in the dirt at the edge of the encampment, the embroidered eagle *vexillum* blew in the faint breeze.

Growing impatient, Titus approached Flavius. "I cannot tolerate anymore setbacks, Flavius. More importantly, as you can see, the gods now favor a move. Is the siege ramp ready?"

"Lieutenant, it may have taken longer than expected, but it's re-buttressed and ready to go!"

"Very well, gather your infantry and make a decisive charge up the ramp. And by the gods, turn this damn rock into rubble if necessary!"

"Yes, sir!" Flavius barked.

With a quicksilver relay of the command, each soldier strapped on their *lorica segmentata* and then eagerly grasped their gladius and large protective *scutum*. As Flavius and his squad stormed up the ramp, their clattering armor and stampeding feet echoed throughout the valley. A fine, dry dust arose in the warriors' wake, as their battle cries reverberated among the valley's chiseled chasms.

Approaching the peak, their echoes gradually subsided, giving way to an eerie silence. Like armored beetles, a few soldiers quietly scaled the large, stoned wall. As they reached the crest, they cautiously crawled on their bellies and then peered down, one by one.

One quickly turned about and cried, "Commander, come here at once! You must take a look at this."

Flavius eagerly began scaling the wall, as two soldiers extended their arms down and hoisted him upward. Unsheathing his gladius, Flavius then crawled beside his comrades and peered down.

Flavius' eyes widened as he sprung to his feet. "Mars be damned! What is this?"

One soldier angrily snarled, "I don't know, sir! But Mars robbed me of filleting these damned troublemakers."

"Me, too!" another soldier balked.

Then in a flurry of bewilderment, the soldiers sounded off in a cacophony of curiosity.

"Did they starve?"

"Could be, we almost did ourselves while we built that damn ramp."

"No, you fools, *look!* They all have been slain!"

One soldier squinted as he tried to focus on the distant bodies below. "You're right! Look at all that blood!"

"I don't get it," another replied.

Flavius slid his pristine gladius back into his scabbard, and then signaled for his remaining unit to approach. He then turned back toward the bloody carnage below. "Well,

I'm guessing they didn't have the rations for such a long siege, but it looks like they killed each other, or possibly even themselves."

"Themselves? But, isn't that against their strange cult, Commander?"

"I believe so," Flavius replied. "I'm fairly certain they're prohibited from committing *desperata salus* (noble suicide). But whatever happened, it certainly looks like their one and only God has forsaken them."

One by one, they crawled down into the huge stronghold. Slowly, they tread through a field of dead bodies, gazing at the self-slaughter in disbelief. Over nine hundred carcasses of men, women, and children lay strewn about, coldly drenched in their own languid pools of blood. As they walked past cadaverous bodies of women and children, with fresh lacerations through their chests and slit throats, some soldiers became furious, while others turned in disgust.

Meanwhile, other soldiers rummaged through the storage chambers and spotted piles of ample rations, magazines of weapons, and even religious artifacts. To their left was a huge golden menorah, and deep into the far corner was a dusty, wooden platform. Two soldiers approached the suspicious grating, as the older of the two, named Antonius, kicked it with his foot.

The younger soldier, Lucas, inquired, "What do you suppose it is?"

"I don't know," Antonius replied. "Perhaps they stored munitions or perishables on it, or maybe performed religious ceremonies here; who knows?"

Lucas smiled. "Well, I know what it's good for!"

Dropping his *scutum*, Lucas quickly grasped the huge menorah and jumped onto the platform. In a juvenile romp, Lucas did a madcap victory dance, while he callously bobbed the menorah over his head. Antonius didn't wish to encourage him, but quite unexpectedly, Lucas slipped. As the menorah rammed Lucas on the head, sending him to his knees, Antonius burst out laughing. Meanwhile, soldiers in the distance shook their heads disparagingly.

But then Antonius turned his head sideways and stopped laughing. "Wait! Did you hear that hollow sound?"

"No," Lucas replied, as he got up and continued his mindless dance. "What hollow sound?"

"Never mind! It probably was your hollow head, you damn fool. Just get down! I want to see what's underneath this grating."

With a perplexed look, Lucas lowered the wobbling menorah and hobbled off the platform. They each grasped opposite ends of the wooden grating and began lifting. Overcome with curiosity, other soldiers entered the chamber and huddled around them.

As Antonius and Lucas flipped over the bulky grating, their eyes widened. There before them, was a hole, approximately eight feet in diameter. Peering down, Antonius could see several dirty faces emerge out of the darkness, looking like trapped animals in a pit. Two women started to climb upward, followed by five children As Antonius and Lucas each extended a hand to help the women up, the children quickly crawled out and clung onto their mothers' soiled tunics.

The women began wailing in Hebrew, as Antonius and Lucas indecisively looked at one another. With a slight understanding of Hebrew, Antonius intently listened to their wrenching story. Meanwhile, he discreetly waved to Lucas to summon Flavius.

As Antonius strained to comprehend their words, it was only moments, when Lucas returned with Flavius right behind. Brushing the soldiers and Lucas aside, Flavius boldly approached Antonius from behind and stared at the survivors. The women were still imparting their tales of woe, when Flavius demandingly interrupted, "What is this? Who are they, and how is it they're still alive?"

Antonius confusedly turned and faced Flavius. "Sir, they were part of the Sicarii tribe. However, when their leader, Eleazar, instructed them to commit suicide, they disobeyed, and silently snuck off. They say at first the tribe refused, but Eleazar's persuasive words slowly cajoled them." Antonius shook his head. "Can you believe it? They did this to themselves."

Flavius' face twisted with disgust as he grumbled, "What a bizarre lot! By the gods, what were they thinking?"

As Antonius stood mute, and innocently shrugged his shoulders, Flavius slowly turned and gazed at all the carnage outside the chamber door. Quickly, he turned back toward Antonius. "Look at all the slain women and children out there. Do you mean to say they actually did this to their own kin, and then themselves?"

"Yes, sir, at least that's what they tell me."

Flavius gazed at the two women. "Well, why didn't *they* kill themselves?"

With a puzzled look, Antonius replied, "Sir, they mentioned something about fearing a Sixth Commandment." Then pointing down at the hole, he added, "So, they sought refuge in this pit."

Flavius looked down into the dark bunker, then back up at Antonius. Pensively he rubbed his chin. "What *is* this Sixth Commandment?"

Antonius shrugged his shoulders. "I don't really know, sir, but perhaps it's a tribal law of some kind. Should I ask them?"

Flavius paused, then shook his head. "Never mind. Obviously, this commandment can't be too commanding. Besides, any tribe that is heartless enough to kill their own kin and then themselves doesn't interest me in the least. Extend my congratulations to these fine women and children for making a wise decision. Then let's gather our gear, and whatever rations or plunder you find here, and report back to Titus."

Many of the soldiers looked at one another and shrugged their shoulders. In bewilderment, they all turned and began rummaging about. As several soldiers exited the chamber, some stepped over the dead bodies, while others stopped to search through the cadavers' pockets or strip them of jewelry. Others walked about and overturned barrels and ceramic jars, and then packed their satchels with dried herbs and other edibles for the long journey home.

Meanwhile, Lucas ran straight over to the golden menorah. He bent over to admire the decorative candelabrum, then awkwardly lobbed it onto his hip. Several soldiers drifted nearby to get a glimpse of the impressive trophy, yet as Lucas struggled to carry the weighty prize, they laughed and began ribbing the lanky youth.

Then with a commanding yell by Flavius, they all regrouped and began to descend the ramp. Halfway down, Flavius and his troops met up with Titus, who was now marching feverishly toward them.

Titus looked up, and barked, "By Jove, what in blazes is going on? I didn't order a retreat!"

Flavius came to a halt. "Lieutenant, this is not a retreat. Actually, I'm not sure how to explain this, but..."

Flavius did his best to relay the odd and harrowing event, while Titus squinted and shook his head. He then ordered Flavius to bring the women captives to the frontline.

As the women and children appeared before him, Titus' eyebrows pinched downward. Filled with curiosity, he turned and addressed one of the women in her Hebrew tongue. "So, what has given you impetus to defy your leader Eleazar?"

The trembling woman looked up at the broad-shouldered commander, as her lower lip quivered. "Sir, when Eleazar spoke of his depraved plan, commanding us to massacre our kin and then ourselves, we immediately knew God's will no longer flowed from his lips. And we—"

"*Subsisto! Satis!*" Titus interrupted. Realizing his intuitive Latin outburst, Titus immediately reverted to Hebrew. "How could *he*, or anyone, accomplish such an outlandish command? What on earth did Eleazar actually say?"

The woman nervously paused to gain her composure. Then quite mysteriously, her eyes rolled up into her head as she stood in an almost trance-like state.

Solemnly, she incanted, "The words of Eleazar are agonizingly etched into my mind, for he said, 'God has convinced us that our hopes were in vain, by bringing such distress upon us in the desperate state we are now in, and which is beyond all our expectations; for the nature of this fortress, which was in itself unconquerable, has not proved a means of our deliverance. And even while we have still great abundance of food, and a great quantity of arms, and other necessaries more than we want, we are openly deprived by God himself of all hope of deliverance.'"

Then, as if awakened from her trance, the woman's eyes rolled downward and fixated upon Titus, as she continued, "It was then that Eleazar proceeded to sway our tribe. For he conveyed unto them the covenant as a reminder, that hitherto only we Jews are entitled to the grace of Yahweh. Hence, all those outside the fortress' walls are wicked, and shall fall, like stone, to their graves. For this self-sacrificial deed, Yahweh would honor his chosen. It was then that our tribe bowed to his will. Yet, bemused my sister and I were, until we pondered this act of sin and desperation; and alas, it was one not to be found in our written laws, hence one not to be fulfilled by our devout deeds."

Titus rolled his eyes and shook his head. "It befuddles me how few of you have a grasp of logic. Only seven, amongst a thousand, placed reason above blind obstinacy. Ever since my father, Vespasian, was a general under Nero, up to his ultimate rise to emperor, of which I soon shall follow, has my family been forced to engage you Jews in this senseless feud. Have we not allowed you soil to build your temples? Do we not permit you to worship freely? Have we not built marketplaces to assist you in trade?"

As the woman stood petrified and mute, Titus continued, "How is it that when my father was honored with the title of emperor even foreign nations sent embassies to congratulate him, yet you ungrateful wretches decided to plot a revolt instead? Do you not see that only a small portion of Rome's many legions are required to manage your limited numbers? Can you not see that no other nation would be foolhardy enough to embrace your cause, especially against the might of Rome? You arrogant lot, who prosper from our resources, while staying unto yourselves, only to spurn or denigrate others who are *not chosen*, and this, all the while under the protection of Rome's mighty sword. Is it your perpetual desire to shun assimilation, and fight the hand that protects?"

Fear was etched upon the woman's face as growing beads of perspiration navigated their way down the crevices of her weathered face. With trembling lips, she uttered, "Lieutenant Titus, our tribe despised your master, Nero, with much passion, and with good reason. He was a wicked man, even by Roman standards—as all of Rome celebrated his death and tore down his Golden House. And Eleazar believed you and your father to be of the same vile blood."

Titus sniggered. "Well, my lady, my Flavian lineage is the first to break free of the Julio-Claudian bloodline. So we quite literally share no blood with our predecessors. Moreover, my father despised Nero, and has every intention of turning this empire back to the Golden Age, which Augustus had miraculously established. Quite sadly, most of his descendants failed to follow his noble precedent."

The woman's tense shoulders lowered. "Of that, time will tell, Lieutenant. But you must know, our religion dictates that we follow no authority but that of our own Lord God."

Titus crossed his muscular arms and gazed into her eyes with profound curiosity. "And what did your Lord God say to you atop that monolithic altar—that your own despotic leader, Herod, built ages ago and almost touches the heavens itself?"

The woman stood silent as her shoulders wilted.

Titus shook his head. "Ah, yes, there is no need for an answer. Is there? Eleazar's oration, and the final conclusion, both speak for themselves."

Impulsively, Titus turned toward his troops. "My fellow Romans, you see before you the end result of what happens to rebels who choose not to respect Roman law, or assimilate into our rich heritage. Radical nonconformists have no place in civilization, and shall perish by the sword, or as you see here today, ill fortune. Divine providence continues to shine upon us, while a dark shroud shall vex these bands of terrorists until they realize the errors of their ways. We offered them freedom of religion, they chose ingratitude; we offered them free trade, they chose treachery; we offered them protection, and they chose rebellion."

The soldiers began to cheer, as Titus continued, "You see before you a tribe that despises us for making mistakes, as if they are pure and flawless. Yet they even defiled their own religion to become terrorists, using their daggers to kill innocent Romans in public marketplaces, and as you see here today, even ignored their god to commit suicide."

As the soldiers simmered, with eyes glued to Titus' commanding presence and rousing oration, Titus continued,

"Or perhaps they despise us for our greatness out of pure jealousy. It is fine for them to build temples and control their flock, yet they grow bitter at Rome's colossal might that robs them of their rank. Yet, all Rome sought was modest tribute, which in turn gave them free passage to our commerce and culture, and of course unmatched security. Yes, the security to practice their cult unmolested by outside invaders. For Roman law had been the most accommodating to the Jewish sect, more so than any other—allowing them to prohibit even Roman citizens from entering their holy temples. Make no mistake...in the final analysis these wretched souls of Masada chose resignation, we inspiration. They chose cowardice, we courage. They chose death, we life!"

The troops broke out into a hysterical roar of jubilation as Titus yelled, "Once again, my brethren, Rome is victorious!"

The troops rallied around Lucas, then lifted the huge menorah above their heads. Triumphantly, they paraded their trophy down the ramp, shouting repeatedly, *"Victoria! Victoria!..."*

❄   ❄   ❄

The Masada event was a significant and well-documented moment in history. Details of the siege were provided by contemporary historians, while Eleazar's complete dialogue, relayed here by the Jewish woman, was a direct quote. Minor extracts of dialogue by Titus have likewise been incorporated.

Although Masada has received much attention, it was actually just one historic event amid a momentous time of change. Eleven years later, in AD 84, the triumphant Arch of Titus was erected in the Roman forum. On its surface, detailed carvings recounted many of Titus' victories, including the eventual triumph of his Jewish campaign, which was etched into history's eternal memory. The arch still stands today as testament to Rome's unyielding determination and ability to maintain order regardless of the obstacles.

The colossal ramp they constructed to reach the mountaintop was a reflection of how the Romans were adept at inventing solutions to overcome seemingly unimaginable odds. About a hundred years earlier, Julius Caesar also shocked and awed the Germanic tribes when he fashioned a bridge out of local timber to cross the Rhine. The engineering of Caesar's bridge—with tree trunk pilings thirty feet long, each driven deep into the riverbed on angles to support a heavy timber superstructure—was extremely innovative. Just as miraculous, Julius Caesar's men built that bridge in only ten days. Titus and his men would similarly follow the Roman tradition of never accepting failure, and that unyielding determination was the fuel of their empire.

However, along with their determination, the Romans also displayed leniency and tolerance toward other ethnic and religious groups, particularly toward the Jews. This is revealed in the fact that Jews were granted liberties not offered to other religions or cults. Despite this fact, historians have slandered Romans for centuries, as have many Jews, branding the Romans as intolerant villains, and this makes the incident at Masada worthy of closer attention.

As is well known, the Roman Empire was vast. It was a colorful spectrum of different races and sects, and with the Roman invention of paved roads, they actually shrunk the world. This effectively inaugurated trade on a new and robust level. Yet intense conflicts between religions were on the rise, and unfortunately, Vespasian's predecessor, Nero, often added fuel to the fire. However, Vespasian and Titus boldly stepped to the fore, as if valiant firefighters determined to quench the toxic flames, for their mission was to not only regain order, but also to essentially rescue their civilization, which Augustus and others before them fought so hard to create.

Once Vespasian wrested control of the floundering government, he had to contend with this aberrant Sicarii tribe, which had begun their rampage many years earlier. Therefore, this last pocket of revolt had to be put down, and that meant even in the harshest manner if necessary, for to leave these rogues unchecked would have allowed them to regroup and cause greater havoc or, worse yet, set the example that Rome was anemic and open to revolt by any radical faction.

Not too surprisingly, however, is how Jewish historians have often attempted to retell the Masada event as a Jewish victory. Their interpretation is one of religiously defiant Jews taking their own lives rather than submitting to the oppressive Romans. As noble as that may sound, that, too, bears scrutiny.

First, and most importantly, it defies their core religion. It claims that suicide is permissible by allowing mortals to overrule God's commandment as they see fit. This is clearly against the words of Yahweh, their Lord God. This blasphemy is further backed up in Deuteronomy 27:26 "Cursed be everyone who does not abide by all things written in the book of the law, and do them."

Second, the Sicarii tribe's name actually reveals its identity, and anti-religious intent. The word sica means stiletto or dagger. Hence, this particular Jewish tribe acquired its name for killing, not the peaceful worship of Yahweh. They were a rouge, terrorist tribe, apart from the core Jewish faith.

Third, it insinuates that William Travis, Davy Crockett, and their cohorts at the Alamo, who were also trapped in a fortress, all gallantly fought to their last dying breath in vain.

Namely, that if they took their own lives it would have somehow transformed their plight into victory. Interestingly enough, in this scenario, the side that emerged victorious was that of the slain, for it was the Texans' tenacious United States that eventually prevailed. However, such was not the case for these Sicarii rebels. Yet here the notion of dying with valor is demeaned, while fanatical suicide is hailed as noble.

Considering all these factors, the rationale of those who defend the Sicarii as valiant heroes can only be deemed flawed. In contrast, most historians today firmly conclude that the Sicarii were a small rebel group of Jews who were extreme radicals, or more appropriately, zealots.

This is an interesting and conclusive point. The term zealot was actually coined by the writer Josephus during this exact moment in history. Born into a wealthy family of Jewish priests, Josephus was later put in command of forces to repel Vespasian (Vespasian at the time was a Roman general). However, during that battle, which was also Josephus' military premiere, he appealed to reason and his own sense of morals, and persuaded his rebel guerillas that their mission was futile. Josephus surrendered to Vespasian and spared further bloodshed. He was briefly held in captivity and later released.

Vespasian treated Josephus with clemency, and even granted his freedom, a freedom that enabled him to be a key voice in history. Moreover, Josephus' new term, *zealot*, defined these fanatical Jewish rebels, which he witnessed firsthand, because they fought zealously for God. And to some extent, these zealots were akin to the religious fanatics of present day Jihad. Their extremist bent on suicide—as being an honorable deed for their maligned concept of faith—resounds with unnerving familiarity.

Historic records elucidate how these religious zealots would slip into a crowded square and silently stab their foe, then amid the panic, exit the scene. Or when they were acting as so-called martyrs, they would opt to commit suicide. From a religious viewpoint, it is one thing for a martyr to be executed by a foe, and another when they defy God's Commandment and commit suicide. This fanatical act clearly illustrates how they truly act upon their own accord, and not that of the true Lord they supposedly represent. As such, the importance of Masada should no longer be glorified as the ultimate symbol of Jewish martyrdom, but rather acknowledged as a mass of fanatical suicides by infidels of Yahweh.

In the final analysis, it was Titus who ruled supreme at Masada and beyond, well into his own reign. The noble visions and efforts of Vespasian and Titus had rescued the Roman Empire from completely falling under Nero's abusive term, and had restored order in the religious realm of their multi-ethnic/multi-religious empire.

Arch of Titus
with closeup of Judean victory engraving

HADRIAN: *The Need For Borders*

Dark clouds billowed as a moist gale blew icy droplets into the surrounding trenches. Nearby, mossy bogs became sodden as dank odors emanated into the damp air. The dreary landscape, lined with gnarled trees and knobby hills, made a foreboding impression. In the midst of this desolate place, muddied mules and oxen dutifully labored alongside their human counterparts in their grueling task. Standing nearby in his saturated purple toga, with rain droplets cascading down his face and off his curly beard, was the great Roman emperor, Hadrian.

The year was AD 122. The mighty Caesar was visiting the work site at *Vindolanda* in Britain. Hadrian was the first and only emperor to physically visit all the provinces of the vast empire, which was in the midst of another golden age. Trajan's previous reign, which was marked by many new conquests that expanded the empire to unprecedented limits, had kept the army very busy. But Hadrian's plans were centered more on keeping the peace and building groundbreaking edifices, such as the Pantheon in Rome, which featured the first successful large dome in history. As such, Hadrian did much to elevate the prestige and magnificence of the empire even further. As such, villagers from all sectors often showed their appreciation.

Making a routine inspection, Hadrian walked through the drenched grass and approached his project leader. "Dio, are we secured in getting the proper amount of stone we need?"

"Yes, Caesar, we have managed to quarry the nearby hills. And as you ordered, we are no longer using timber." Dio turned, and proudly pointed. "You see, these walls are now solid stone with two small turrets strategically placed between each milecastle, just as your plans indicate. But, to insure your timeframe, we are carving the stone into small irregular units."

"Very well, so long as this wall fulfills its purpose without fail, I see no reason to construct a masterpiece."

Besides being a competent leader, Hadrian was also an outstanding architect. While touring the empire, Hadrian's photographic memory had captured and analyzed a wealth of architectural data that was creatively utilized to produce some of the empire's most impressive structures. But, for Hadrian, now standing in this damp and desolate land, this immense project was for security, not refined grandeur.

Hadrian scanned the site. "I see the strata are lined with only ten carts, I will see to it that you receive more."

"Thank you, Caesar. But, what I really need is more soldiers." Dio looked discreetly about, then added, "These damn Britons are sufficient laborers, but the ones outside these walls are mindless savages. They ruthlessly attack our workers day and night."

Hadrian nodded. "Yes, that is why I visited your outpost specifically. I've heard of the frequent attacks here, but all I can allot you is one additional legion until this section is complete. After all, I do need to secure other outposts along the wall. Remember, Dio, you are not alone in your efforts to secure Rome. Fellow Romans work along this eighty-milliarium stretch, and they risk their lives daily, as do you, all for the greater cause. I'm sure you can understand that."

Dio looked up and gave a patriotic nod. "Yes, Caesar. I will do my best, and we will not fail you."

Hadrian smiled, then gently grasped Dio's elbow. As he escorted him away from the nearby soldiers and Britons, he added in a hushed voice, "Bear in mind, Dio, that this enterprise has many facets. As I have opted not to follow Trajan's policy of expansion, this wall serves two purposes. First, is to secure our present borders from invasion. But second, I need to keep our soldiers busy." As they continued walking through the mud and rain, Dio squinted, a bit confused at Hadrian's last condition. Meanwhile, Hadrian looked into Dio's eyes, deeply. "These men, Dio, are groomed for the dangerous adventures of combat and glorious conquest, not for idle down time. This is quite possibly the worst condition to befall a military unit. Therefore, while security is essential, so, too, is productivity. The majority of these men need to be transformed into competent builders or simple laborers, while the remainder stands ready for battle. So, don't fear working them too hard, Dio. Fear leaving them to their own destructive devices."

Dio stopped and gazed at Hadrian with an admiring grin. "Yes, Caesar. Your point is well taken and will be implemented with my full devotion."

Hadrian nodded, then slapped him firmly on the shoulder. Dio respectfully pivoted about, and marched straight through the cold drizzle back to his post. Stepping awkwardly over the muddy potholes, Dio looked back at his master with a grin, then pressed his workers onward.

As Hadrian began walking back toward his entourage, a huge figure suddenly appeared from behind a thicket of gnarled trees. Towering at almost seven feet tall, and wielding a large rusty hoe, the behemoth approached Hadrian from behind.

Ten praetorian guards quickly lunged into action. In rapid succession, they unsheathed their swords and encircled the emperor. Hadrian immediately pivoted about, and peered through the silver gate of vertical gladius blades. Wiping the rain out of his eyes, Hadrian strained to take a closer look.

Meanwhile, the gargantuan beast continually plodded forward. Through a thin veil of rain, Hadrian could now see that the disheveled beast had finally stopped dead in his tracks. Taking a defensive posture, the Goliath stood fixed as he gazed at the snarling guards. His dirty, long wet hair and scruffy beard blew in the damp breeze, as Hadrian squinted to observe him closer. As the leading guards took aggressive steps forward, Hadrian noticed the charier expression on the man's face. With a snap of his fingers, Hadrian deactivated the attack, then waved for his guards to step aside. As the praetorians' protective gate opened, the brawny Briton slowly entered the fold.

In a deep, thick accent, he rumbled, "I apologize, me Lord, but I just felt 'twas me duty to impart to ya that it's an honor for all of Vindolanda to welcome ya to our humble village."

Hadrian gazed upward into the pouring rain to connect eye to eye, blinking as the water pounded his face. "The pleasure is mine, good man. So, what do you Vindolandians think of my wall?"

As their eyes glanced at the workers chiseling stone and taking measurements, the Brit replied, "We think it be a grand thing, Caesar. We here know how to slash a tree for timber, but stone be another matter. You Romans do some fine things with it."

Hadrian nodded. "Yes, we've been crafting stone and marble for many centuries and have made the mundane an art. The Greeks and Egyptians have done some marvelous work with stone, too. So I'm rather surprised not to find much use of it up here."

Well, me Lord, its somethin' we ought to start learnin'. In fact, we've been gatherin' materials from far and wide to assist buildin' this wall as best we can." The giant's face turned solemn. "Ya see, me Lord, I lost me two brothers and me wife to these marauders. Them bloody mules just attack ar village and farms without cause. All we wish do is put food on ar tables, and mind ar own flock. Yet, now I alone remain to rear me five children." His face contorted with rage. "They're nothin' but bloody bastards! All of them!"

Hadrian wiped the rain out of his eyes. "That, my good man, is exactly why I made this visit! I assure you, it's my firm intent to secure you and your families from hostile invasion and pillage." Hadrian's head rotated, doing a 180 degree sweep of the precarious horizon, as he continued, "I've received word that these barbarians have killed, raped, and plundered your people, and *that*, I'll have you know, is *not* acceptable." Gazing back up into the giant's big blue eyes, he added, "Rome insures the protection of its entire population, no matter where they reside. And once this project is complete, I intend to have ten thousand troops stationed along the entire breadth of this wall, which runs from coast to coast, spanning your entire island."

The Briton's eyes widened upon hearing the immense scale of the project. "I had no idea, me Lord, no idea at all that such a thing could be done! Me thought this wall would flank ar own village." Humbly, he bowed his head. "Many thanks, me Lord, many thanks indeed. We be much obliged."

As the emperor and Briton made small talk, the praetorian guards impatiently peered up at the ever-darkening sky and then back down at the chatting duo.

Meanwhile, several yards away, a young Roman soldier, whose lips were as purple as Hadrian's toga, turned to his older comrade, and moaned; "This godforsaken place is too damn wet and cold for me, Bracus. I can't wait to get back home."

Bracus chuckled. "Well, Adrian, that's not going to happen anytime soon. You know Hadrian, he's going to have us touring the whole damn world before we get back to Rome."

A wiry guard standing nearby overheard Adrian's complaint, and bounced in front of him. "Hey, *parum puer* (little boy)! This is a journey of a lifetime. We've had the good fortune of seeing the provinces of Gaul and the Rhineland. Many soldiers have been permanently stationed with little or nothing to do. Besides, after Briton, Hadrian has many other destinations planned. So, I suggest you join the party or get your whimpering ass transferred!"

Bracus, stepped forward. "Don't worry *perturbo plasmator* (trouble maker), Adrian will pull his weight. And from the size of this project, I don't think we'll be leaving this soggy, frigid island anytime soon."

The ornery soldier stood firm, and was ready to exchange fists, but Bracus clutched Adrian by his bony arm and quietly walked him away.

Adrian peered up and whispered, "What an asshole!"

As Bracus laughed, Adrian suddenly slipped and fell into a gooey bog. Turning about, Bracus began laughing even louder, as the boy sat covered in mud and moss.

Adrian gazed up at the sky and groaned, "Jove! Have mercy! Get us out of this stinking urinal." Then gazing at

Bracus, he cried, "Even Aeneas and Romulus would have abandoned this place!"

Meanwhile, back near the emperor, the praetorians had grown restless, as one sternly intervened, "Caesar, the Imperial chariot awaits you. We do have many other stops to make, and this terrain is almost saturated. Remember, Caesar, there are no roads in this Celtic wilderness!"

The brawny Briton was suddenly aware; his time with the busy emperor had expired. Nervously, he quickly bowed his head, then awkwardly turned to depart. But before he took another step, he stopped and looked back. "Ah, yeah, me Lord, we'd also like to thank ya for honor'n ar people by puttin' Britannia on the new Denarius. That means a great deal ta us. Britannia has long been ar Lady of hope."

Hadrian smiled. "Yes, so long as it's Britannia, and not Boudica!"

The praetorian guards burst out with sinister cackles, while others vengefully hissed, not appreciating being reminded of the British woman-warrior that had wreaked havoc on Roman legions many years ago. The huge Briton planted himself firmly, with fists drawn, as his eyes carefully gazed at the metal-clad warriors from side to side.

Hadrian stepped over and patted the Briton on the back. "Now, now, never mind this pernicious pack of praetorians; they're just my personal watchdogs." Hadrian pointed to the work site. "Those stalwart soldiers building the wall over there are the ones you need to look at. They're the ones who are stationed here to protect *you*, Vindolanda, and all of civilized Briton." Noticing that the Brit was still fixated on the praetorians, Hadrian thought it best to switch topics. "Have you had a chance to see our magnificent baths and villas scattered about these lands?"

With his eyes still locked on the praetorians, the giant replied cautiously, "No, me Lord, but me friends have, and they do say they're grand, grand indeed."

Hadrian smiled, "Yes, grand they are, and hopefully once these walls are up we can build more villas that will make production and wealth here rival even Rome itself. What do say about that?"

The Briton's tense shoulders lowered as he finally turned and released a big smile. With his huge, yellow teeth veering crookedly out of his gums, he replied, "That would be grand! But, I have to tell ya, me Lord, all I've been fixin' on doin' is learnin' how to build me a cart, like ye Romans. I got to carry me crops all about on horseback." He pointed to his decrepit horse, standing several feet behind him. "But that feeble old mare can't carry much, 'specially bein' able ta carry only two small pouches. And she complains, too, she does." He gazed at her with evil eyes, and uttered, "You just may end up bein' dinner, lassy!"

As Hadrian laughed, the Briton added dryly, "Laugh all ya like, me Lord, but if ya have a good recipe for horse stew, be sures ta let me know!?"

Hadrian chuckled. "Well, we Romans have no recipes for horse meat, but I *will* have one of our engineers give you a hand building that cart." As Hadrian and the Brit stepped through the rain and mud while lightning flashed in the distance, Hadrian scanned all the Britons laboring alongside the Romans. He came to a stop and gazed at them admiringly, then up at the giant by his side, who also stopped. "You're a good man, and so, too, is this a good village. So you're all entitled to Rome's expertise and protection. The barbarians outside these walls, on the other hand, only seek to destroy all we build, worship, and cherish. They are not like you or I, now are they?"

The Briton looked down at Hadrian's sincere expression as a warm grin etched his weather-beaten face. "No, me Lord, nothin' like us."

"Very well then, you have nothing to fear. Our walls and soldiers will take care of securing Vindolanda, while you can go on and build your cart. Just remember, you and I both desire the same things, prosperity and safety. And by the gods, they will be ours!"

Hadrian glanced at the praetorian guards and waved his hand, as they impatiently escorted him to the royal chariot. Hadrian looked up at the dark, misty sky as he climbed aboard. As he turned back, the Briton grabbed his old horse by the rein, and proudly signaled a salute. With a crack of the whip, Hadrian's chariot bucked and rolled forward.

As the Briton looked on with veneration, the sounds of busy hammers and chisels discordantly clashed with the clamor of thunder and rain. Awash with a feeling of contentment, the Briton gently patted his horse, then turned to look her straight in the eye. "Don't worry, love, ya wouldn't taste good any hows."

As the horse snorted, he gazed back up. Suddenly he noticed a warm hazy clearing upon the distant horizon. Serenely, he watched as Hadrian's chariot receded over the husky hills and into the dewy drapes of dusk.

❊　❊　❊

Hadrian's visit to Briton demonstrates a concerned ruler physically overseeing a serious threat and implementing a practical solution. The wall's impressive specifications mentioned in this vignette were factual, as were some other details, such as the number of soldiers that Hadrian would station there. Furthermore, the Briton had good reason to be nervous at the mention of Boudica, for she happened to be a warrior queen from Briton's past.

Boudica had led a vicious campaign against the Romans while under Nero's rule. Nero's avaricious bent for over-taxation forced her to rally local tribes and they slaughtered thousands of Romans. In retaliation, Nero supplied the Roman governor with new legions that commandingly annihilated the insurgents and reestablished order.

Julius Caesar had been the first Roman to ever attempt the conquest of Briton, as it sat only twenty-two miles across the sea, and must have piqued his curiosity. When his mission failed, Caesar rightfully complained that the population was larger than expected, thus the reason why his limited forces couldn't accomplish the task. Some later historians claimed that Caesar was simply trying to make excuses in order to maintain his perfect record, yet recent discoveries have validated Caesar's claims, as the population was much larger than most historians realized.

However, under the rule of Emperor Claudius, a renewed attempt of conquest was made in AD 43, and after several decades, all of lower Briton fell under Roman rule. With Nero succeeding Claudius, it was under Nero's regime that the continued attacks mounted to complete the task. However, once Briton was conquered, Nero's greed and lack of public relations only instilled resentment and eventually vengeance. Unfortunately, anything touched by Nero's sulfuric hands exploded into volatile flames, be it his dealings with the Jews, the Christians, or the Britons. Nero's bloody fourteen-year rule was painfully brutal, but transient. Although he caused a great deal of havoc and significant shifts in world history, Nero had also procured a tidal wave of bias over the centuries that many historians used to drown the entire empire in shame.

However, after Nero's death, Vespasian ordered the highly competent general Agricola to manage Briton. *(Agricola also happened to be the father-in-law of Tacitus, the leading Roman historian of the age.)* Agricola conquered almost all of Briton yet was stopped from completing the task by the then reigning emperor, namely Vespasian's second son, Domitian. Agricola also happened to be a superb peacetime administrator and was extremely influential in Romanizing Briton. This not only included building roads, houses, villas, baths, and temples, but Agricola also ensured that all the sons of prominent Britons were educated in the liberal arts. This was the foundation of ingraining Latin into Briton and why the future English language has Latin as its root. In fact, almost two-thirds of the English language is made up of Latin words, not to mention how English uses the Roman alphabet, hence the words you're reading right now.

Nevertheless, the times and treatment of Britons had changed, particularly under Hadrian, who took a personal interest in every region throughout the empire. Hadrian authorized many projects during his vast travels, including urban developments in Libya, Athens, or even his timber blockade along the troublesome Germanic border, for his architectural signature is to be found in almost every province.

Along with these ventures came new knowledge and progress, as carpenters living in timber and mud villages, such as in Briton, slowly learned stone and mortar construction. Additionally, hydro technologies were adopted along with architectural and agricultural tools and apparatus, which were either invented or improved upon by the Romans. Hence, the positive influence of ancient Rome permeates numerous European, North African, and some Middle Eastern and Asian nations. And one of the emperors who significantly aided in that grand endeavor was Hadrian. Besides having been competent at military and political tasks, Hadrian has been credited with having a hand in designing many of the sophisticated architectural wonders created during his reign, including the Pantheon and Hadrian's Villa, which became the template for most future royal gardens. And paramount to protecting this rich culture was the necessity of building Hadrian's Wall.

CONSTANTINE: *Christianity's Most Powerful Advocate*

Under a thick blanket of gray clouds, the air was moist and motionless. Suddenly a mysterious turbulence split the clouds as a celestial beam of light pierced through the cumulus mist like a divine rapier.

Riding in full battle regalia was Constantine, one of the three remaining rulers of Diocletian's crumbling tetrarchy that had turned into a triumvirate. The year was AD 312, and Constantine, along with his legions, was approaching the Milvian Bridge, just outside Rome. It was at this precise moment that the pagan ruler witnessed an apparition that would not only alter his beliefs but also miraculously change world history forever.

As the clouds parted, Constantine beheld a startling vision—a cross of light in the sky that beckoned: *By this sign you will be victorious.*

That night, Constantine had a dream in which Christ appeared and instructed him to use the sign of the X and P in the form of a cross on all his battle standards, X and P being the first two letters of the name Christ in Greek. (Greek had become the chosen language of the new gentile believers of Christ, who upon infiltrating the faith dispensed with its Jewish-rooted languages. However, that would all change, for once Constantine fully seized the religion, Latin would become the religion's official language.)

The next day, Constantine inaugurated this symbolic cross, or labarum, by ordering his men to use ash from burned sticks to inscribe the iconograph on their shields and helmets. Equipped with this divine symbol, Constantine effectively dominated his rival and former co-emperor, Maxentius. It was a victory of prophetic proportions, but only the first of many heaven and earth-shattering changes that would soon follow.

Although this colorful tale is riddled with divine drama, for Constantine's close bishop friend and author, Eusebius, penned it into history many years later, the essence of Constantine's physical action was historically profound. First, Constantine's use of the cross as a divine symbol to motivate and unite his Roman troops was strikingly new, for not only was his army mainly pagan, but previously the cross had only been associated with horrific torture and suffering. Even though Saint Paul had made the initial attempt to portray Jesus' suffering as redemption, Christianity itself was still based upon and branded by the peaceful waters of baptism, which soothingly welcomed newcomers into its congregation.

Prior to Constantine, imagery of Jesus had portrayed the Messiah as a young peaceful shepherd. However, after

Constantine, Jesus became the ultimate martyr, nailed to the cross with a golden halo illuminating his divinity, or sitting in a pagan "emperor-like" fashion with a halo. These depictions were all adopted from Roman and even earlier pagan cultures, for the Jewish tradition, which the early Christians still adhered to, shunned graven images or idolatry. This long tradition dated back to Moses and the Ten Commandments, which directly referred to the strange and bizarre idols worshiped in Egypt at that time.

With the advent of Constantine, all this effectively changed, and quite remarkably, his victories established the cross not only as Christianity's new and ultimate icon, but one that was eagerly embraced and admired by pagans as well. As for the spiritual emphasis of the religion, it permanently switched over to the suffering and resurrection of Jesus who died for the sins of mankind.

However, those changes had occurred after Constantine's long reign, for much strife and infighting had besieged the religion previously. Not being the solidified entity it would later become, the religion was splintered into many rivaling sects, each with their own interpretations of the Jesus story and divine message.

As such, thirteen years after Constantine's miraculous vision and conversion at the Milvian Bridge, the Roman emperor decreed that an ecumenical council be gathered in Nicaea. The year was AD 325.

Constantine's Nicaean Council

The huge chamber slowly filled with over three hundred bishops from all parts of the empire. Although there were several adversarial factions in attendance, such as the Donatists, the two main rivals were Arius and Alexander, both men hailing from Alexandria, Egypt.

As the bishops sat awaiting the emperor, they noticed the arrival of three of Constantine's relatives, who in turn were closely followed by a few Christian friends of the imperial family.

Finally, the moment arrived, as Constantine entered the chamber. All the bishops rose to their feet.

As the Roman historian/bishop Eusebius would later record, the emperor entered "like some heavenly angel of God, his bright mantle shedding luster like beams of light, shining with the fiery radiance of a purple robe, and decorated with the dazzling brilliance of gold and precious stones."

Constantine was out to impress, and he looked more like a shining apparition than a mere mortal master of ceremonies. Constantine signaled with his hand, as the two guards remaining inside slowly closed the huge chamber doors. The bishops sighed with relief. They were glad to see only the emperor's family and close associates, rather than an imperial entourage flanked by soldiers.

Constantine strode energetically toward the head of the chamber and then stepped upon a richly decorated marble platform. A fabulously ornate golden chair awaited. Looking like a statuesque relic of Jupiter, Constantine stood majestically while the bishops courteously beckoned him to sit. As the emperor slowly took his seat, the bishops respectfully followed suit.

Constantine briefly scanned the assemblage and began his opening remarks. "It was once my chief desire, dearest friends, to enjoy the spectacle of your united presence; and now that this desire is fulfilled, I feel myself bound to render thanks to God the universal King, because, in addition to all his other benefits, he has granted me a blessing higher than all the rest, in permitting me to see you, not only all assembled together, but all united in a common harmony of sentiment."

The rivaling factions of bishops silently looked at one another with skeptical eyes and somewhat embarrassed hearts, as Constantine continued, "I trust you all shall soon realize the intent, nay, the magnitude of this blessed meeting—that is, of course, after I present my divine plan."

A dissonant murmur rose to a mild rumble, for several Donatist bishops abhorred hearing the pagan emperor speak of *his* divine plan. Although Constantine had openly declared his conversion to Christianity, many questioned his fidelity, as his political actions had appeared to favor a variety of religions, or cults, which permeated the ethnically diverse empire.

With utter calm and restraint, Constantine's big olive eyes hawkishly scanned the audience. In a deep and authoritative voice he summoned, "Anyone who does not feel at one with this task, please stand and speak now."

One by one, the irritated bishops uneasily gazed at one another and unhappily swallowed their grievances. With silence restored, Constantine squarely proceeded, "Men, it is imperative that we act as a single component, with a common spirit of peace and concord. This will be, I assure you, a glorious day for Rome's future. You all have seats on the most important council the world shall ever know. I now place in your most trustworthy hands the foundation of this enormous enterprise, which you all shall take part in constructing. Therefore, much of your knowledge and energy is vital to our success. I am, however, displeased with your unresolved conflict regarding the nature of Jesus. Some of you claim that the scriptures never indicated that Jesus was divine, but only a messenger of God. As we all know, Arius of Alexandria—sitting before me—advocates such a claim."

Arius rose swiftly to his feet. "If I may, Emperor. I once again state my case for the record. The gospels of Matthew, Luke, and Mark, which most here will agree are authoritative, clearly state that Jesus was the *Son* of God and our Messiah. *Not* that he was "God the Father" who resides in heaven. Jesus always spoke of his Father, not as if himself, but as a true and separate being."

Alexander quickly rose in opposition. "Those three gospels may be authoritative, Arius, but so, too, is the most highly regarded gospel, the Gospel of John. Irenaeus had rightfully placed John ahead of your three gospels, yet you defiantly relegate John to last place, or worse yet, omit him completely. This omission is intolerable, for John clearly stated that Jesus is one and the same as God above!"

Arius' head cocked sideways, as he heatedly countered, "God, as we all know, has *always* existed. That clearly means beyond the past and beyond the future, in a word *eternal!* However, there was a time when Jesus did NOT exist, and this, my friends, instantly negates his oneness with God the Father, *and* his alleged divinity!"

Alexander's devout secretary, Athanasius, known for his pit bull temper, lunged to his feet. "Arius, you fool! The Christian faith is this: there is a Father eternal, a Son eternal, and a Holy Ghost eternal, and yet they are not three eternals, but one. If you cannot comprehend this, you have no place here among *true* Christians!"

Constantine's iron hand firmly slapped the golden arm of his chair, prompting the startled bishops to turn and gaze at the emperor in silence. "Men! Sit, and bite your flailing tongues," Constantine commanded. "It is my fervent desire that this council come to terms, standardize the religion, and resolve this conflict, which you must realize in the grand scheme of things, is obstructing progress. As I had stated in my direct written memo, I now state here publicly for all to hear and comprehend. And this communiqué, my good bishops, is not in some lost scroll that may have failed to reach your office, but comes direct from the emperor's mouth. So, *no* excuses will be tolerated!" Constantine leaned forward, and with a stern expression, commanded, "Jesus *was* one and the same as God the Father. John *saw* and *knew* this, and there is one thing I certainly do know. A god commands more power, and attracts more followers than a mere prophet. Therefore, Jesus *must* be God, and *this* the people of Rome *must know!*"

Arius' nostrils flared, as he and his followers boiled silently with rage. Sharing their contempt, were the Donatists and other opposing sects. Meanwhile, Alexander and Athanasius, along with their significantly larger congregation, beamed.

Constantine boldly continued, "Additionally, it is my strong belief that the framework of Christianity must be broadened to embrace some aspects of pagan tradition. Open up your minds and your hearts. Only under such magnanimity of spirit will you be able to weave these pagan threads into the rich fabric of the Christian church. Hence, this task exceeds catering only to Christians, and extends outward; to entice, enlighten, and envelop all the various cults within this great empire. It is my desire that our entire empire, from north and south, and from east and west, shall be united into one solid cross. So, burn this image into your minds. The empire must and *will* be unified. That, my friends, is the miracle I seek from this most eminent council."

Arius and the Donatists turned toward Alexander and Athanasius, and heatedly triggered a spark of revolt. The polyphony of voices soon escalated into a crescendo of chaotic dissonance. Vehement shouts led some to viciously elbow their rivals, as pandemonium ensued.

Just then, a piercing metallic clash painfully shrilled throughout the chamber. Momentarily panic-stricken, the bishops all turned to locate its source. Suddenly, their eyes beheld the culprit. One of the guards had violently slapped his gladius against his breastplate, and was now seething like a wild boar. With a primal grunt, the metal-clad warrior viciously lunged forward and barked, "Order! Take heed! You stand before Caesar!"

The Donatists stood fixed, yet the Catholics and centrists grew evermore anxious as they awaited a reprisal. Still seated on his golden throne, Constantine glared at the guard and raised his hand in disapproval. The emperor then turned toward the council, and spoke in a loud and demanding voice, "Men, I welcome discussion, but you *must* appeal to reason and civility. If I wanted to start a war I would have convened this council on the battlefield, but alas, this was supposed to be a gathering of our most exalted minds. So, I beseech you, pause for a moment to collect your sense of reason—reason guided by Almighty God above—so we may proceed in an orderly manner." Constantine paused, and then eyed the assemblage. With the bishops silently reflecting upon the emperor's words, Constantine added, "That said, is there anyone among you who wishes to speak?"

At the center of the council, an elderly Catholic bishop feebly stood up. "Caesar, I think I speak for all when I say we truly thought this council was formed to assist us in strengthening our own congregations. It is our mission to establish true faith in our God, as told by the Son of God, Jesus Christ. But this monumental task of which you speak is truly another matter. Three hundred years of discord among us bishops coupled with this new task of weaving a universal tapestry is beyond human endeavor. There are countless cults and rituals that need to be considered here, and we cannot even resolve our own internal disputes."

A feisty Donatist bishop sharply rose to his feet, and indignantly barked at Constantine, "And what has the church to do with the emperor?"

The congregations' eyes all darted toward the brazen Donatist, then anxiously back toward Constantine. The ire of the emperor was sparked and Constantine sprang to his feet. "Councilmen! Know this, I, too, am a bishop ordained by God to oversee whatever is external to the church. So, *this* emperor standing before you, dear councilmen, has *everything* to do with the church. You have continued to quarrel amongst yourselves without resolution for three centuries. *Three centuries!* This is something I, as a Roman, cannot accept, nor will I tolerate. Rome's success has always been predicated upon the importance of organization and maintaining unity and order. Rome is clearly torn these days because of your hostility and dissension. Through me, the true servant of God, even the barbarians know God and have learned to reverence him, while you bishops do nothing but that which encourages discord and hatred, and to speak frankly, which leads to the destruction of the human race. As such, I will, nay, *we* will mend this broken foundation, so the road to the future will shine with hope, rather than hostility."

The imprudent Donatist discreetly took his seat as Constantine continued, "Remember this, my brothers; our empire is like a chariot—it can only ride securely over tightly interlocked stones, for over randomly fractured rock, it will surely falter and fall."

One by one, many bishops began to applaud and cheer.

Alexander smiled and glanced around the chamber as he declared, "Yes, my brothers, by mending this road it shall lead us, and our Christian faith, into a secure position. Loose gravel is useless, but cemented together it can pave the way to a glorious future. Let us begin to build this road, here today!"

Constantine nodded graciously, then composedly took his seat. "Very well, it is imperative that we move forward with bold and decisive moves. First, you must resolve these discrepancies regarding the true nature of Jesus. His mortal connotations, once again, seem a hindrance to this grand and noble cause. I advocate full confirmation that Jesus was indeed a supreme being, so one day all of Rome shall worship in unison."

The attending factions were primarily separated into three main groups: those that believed Jesus was a mortal prophet; the monophysites who believed that Jesus was of one nature, both God and man; and those who believed Jesus was of two separate natures, one human and one divine.

A Donatist bishop angrily turned toward Constantine, and shouted, "This in itself is mayhem! We will not compromise our beliefs. Not for any of these wayward sects, or any political agenda."

Without acknowledging the heckler, Constantine calmly looked at the assemblage with a paternal glance. "Know this; dissension is the work of the devil, and strife within the church is far more evil and dangerous than any kind of war."

As the bishops turned and looked at one another, Constantine continued, "We all must recognize that since the very beginning of time, man has divided himself into two distinct factions, those of good and those of evil. And you here are making this distinction amongst yourselves. Some of you look at your brethren and misguidedly summon the sacred words, *denounce Satan*. But I say open your eyes and hearts to see that there are no demons here today. And if you demonize your rival, I beseech you to embrace another verse from your scriptures, "Love thy enemy as thy self." For this alleged enemy you see standing before you is but your Christian brother, and fellow son of God. So, think of the greater cause, and resolve your differences, lest private animosity interfere with God's business. And the order of business here today is to mend a splintered Christianity into a single unified whole. For Christianity remains only a small seed in Rome, a seed that will either wither and die, or blossom and grow. And as the Invincible Sun, my divine light, ordained by Almighty God above, will ensure your growth and influence in the days and years ahead."

Many in the congregation silently digested the emperor's wise words, while others belligerently turned and continued quarreling, for they abhorred his use of the pagan Sun god in the same breath as the one and only true God, Jesus Christ. Tempers flared, and instantaneously a flock of bishops began ramming their fingers into their rival's chests, as they mete out a viral tongue-lashing. Looking like birds in a wild cockfight, the feisty bishops snapped their furious beaks, seeking personal victory for their proprietary faith.

Meanwhile, Constantine's powerful fingers dug into the arms of his chair, as the bishops' vile excoriations echoed throughout the densely packed chamber. But then the emperor's patience died, as he slapped both hands on the arms of his golden chair! "Men of God? I think not. You act like animals! Are you truly that blind to the errors of your ways?"

Many bishops fell silent, as a wave of shame washed over them. Meanwhile, Arius and the Donatists turned and ratcheted down their temper, yet only a few notches.

Alexander stood firm, then pushed his way through the cantankerous crowd. "Yes, Caesar, I concur, it can be done!"

The entire council turned and peered at their Egyptian brother, who intrepidly continued, "We may need to discard some existing scrolls, but I have many scribes that can draft new ones. I agree, we must and will seek a resolution. As you say, too much rides on this not to, and Jesus, our Almighty Father, demands this of us."

Constantine's tense arms and tightly clasped lips gradually relaxed. As the blood slowed in his veins, he calmly leaned forward. "It would be wise if you all share in Alexander's sense of reason."

Constantine's large eyes slowly scanned the simmering council. Exhausted, he leaned back in his golden chair. Placing his elbow on the gilded arm, he tilted his head and rested it on his fingertips. As his eyelids closed, his massive fingers slid up to massage his temple. After a brief moment, his huge eyelids slowly opened. "Let us proceed on the premise that you shall, in some fashion, deify Jesus, and that his nature will be homoousios."

One bishop squinted, as he cried out, "What is homoousios?"

Another echoed, "Homoousios? That word is not to be found anywhere in our scriptures!"

Constantine rolled his eyes, and slowly leaned forward. "It means *of one substance*. And this word *will* be incorporated into scripture here today. Bear in mind that you will need to clearly document all facets of Christ's unique creation and resurrection without any shadow of suspicion."

A short stocky bishop quickly rose to his feet. "Since we have no clear date for the birth of Jesus perhaps we should devise a conception plan similar to the god Mithras or Sol Invictus. If our task is to make the conversion process easy for pagans, then we should be mindful of their current rituals and days of worship. We all know how the masses are reluctant to change."

Scores of bishops huffed, yet one enthusiastic soul leapt to his feet. "Yes, syncretism has helped the transmutation of many other religions, so why not ours as well? We can easily adopt from the entrenched religions, many of which share important dates. As we know, the births of Mithras and Sol Invictus are celebrated on December 25. And the winter solstice has been a mainstay to countless religions and astrologers since the beginning of time. Therefore, if we establish December 25 as Jesus' birth date, there will be no need to change any current celebrations. Life and ritual will continue right on schedule."

One young Donatist swiftly turned, and blasted, "This is hogwash! Have you all gone mad? Do you even hear what you're saying? In lieu of heeding the apostles, you are engaging in the deceptive arts of appropriation and fabrication!"

Another bishop, looking like Jupiter with his thick gray hair and beard, firmly stood up, and retorted, "My poor man, you are nothing but a naïve and unworldly fool! It is an undeniable fact that most religions have appropriated important events and beliefs from their predecessors or rivals, and our cherished Gospels are no different. Any learned man here knows that the Jesus story already mimics that of other deities in certain respects, and our own apostles searched long and hard into ancient Hebrew scriptures to make Jesus fit into tradition, such as his divinity being foretold by Isaiah and others. The past always offers a solid foundation for new enterprises. After all, Mithras was called the *Son of God* and the *Light of the World*, while Horus was called the *Lamb of God* and the *Son of Man* long before Jesus. And where do you think John adopted his concept of Jesus the Son being one and the same as God the Father? Did you really think that concept was original? Nay! It was from the Egyptian god Horus. Horus had become one and the same as his father Osiris. So John's odd and vivid account has a precursor, one that originated thousands of years earlier in ancient Egypt."

As many turned and gasped, the wise old bishop continued, "Those of you who are younger, or simply unread, probably are unaware of these facts, which are more than merely coincidental. Yet the core mission has always been survival. So, be advised, *all* religions have pilfered. Moreover, the ignorance of the masses has always been to the wise man's advantage. So I am actually pleased that some of you are in the shadows, for that certainly means the uneducated masses shall remain in the dark as well. And given that our scriptures have no exact date for Jesus' birth, death, or resurrection, anything we bishops decide can be implemented with divine perfection."

Constantine was impressed, as he smiled and politely clapped. "Yes, I knew brilliance was to be found in this room. Indeed, adoption and transition must be paramount in our endeavors."

While some bishops smoldered and moaned, others began to beam. One bishop energetically rose from the rear of the chamber. He looked more like a bookworm than a bishop, and his nearsightedness made the council look like a blur, yet his vision was crystal clear. "Actually, this adoption and transference resounds with unnerving truth the longer it is subjected to scrutiny. After all, most religions, in one form or another, possess underlying traits of their predecessors, including the ancient mystics and astrologers. The Sun has always been worshiped, from Horus, Ra, and Amun-Ra, to Sol Invictus. As mentioned, even our beloved Jesus Christ has been called the *Light of the World.* So we actually continue to worship the Sun, or *light of the world,* but only with different names and different tales to embellish it. And no one can deny that the ancient astronomers who charted the sun passing through the heavens is the central reason why the number twelve has had so much influence on us, such as the twelve constellations, the twelve signs of the zodiac, the twelve months, the twelve Olympian gods, the twelve tribes of Israel, and now our twelve disciples. Quite interestingly, only the three synoptic gospels mention twelve disciples, John's gospel only mentions nine, of whom one disciple Nathanael was not one of those mentioned by the other three gospels."

As his peers looked on, some with intense interest and others in angst, he continued, "Additionally, not having in our possession the actual scripts of the gospels, but only copies, we can't really be sure if there were actually twelve apostles at all. But we must confess that with all the recurring similarities to the words found in the Torah and all these ancient pagan cults, they certainly didn't commit anything to scripture that was earth-shatteringly new, and in that regard, nothing offensive enough to make us fight amongst ourselves."

The frail-framed bishop gazed at the blurry assemblage around him and offered a congenial smile, as he added, "The underlying force of the heavenly God is what we should acknowledge as being most important and most precious. So I see no reason why we shouldn't continue the tradition of syncretism, as long as we do so with divine purpose to honor the Almighty God, who art in heaven."

Constantine nodded with admiration. "Excellent! And to all of you, this do heed: that I applaud your religion's ability to adapt. This calls to mind Saint Paul and his aptitude for enhancing scripture, as well as his wise decision to target the Roman gentile population. His efforts made significant advances; yet don't be fooled, after two hundred years your numbers still remain scant, and more importantly you still remain splintered. Hence, without my divine guidance your steps will be limited. Believe me, I had served with all those who previously held power, and none embraced your cult, at least not with the zeal that I have been blessed with. And this, I assure you, is because I have been chosen by the Almighty God above to guide us forward. It was His divine will that directed my campaigns to eliminate my competition, and why I alone stand before you as Caesar. Like Saint Paul's vision on the road to Damascus, I, too, have been summoned by the Almighty Father. For the Lord purposefully guided my sword at the Milvian Bridge to oversee our future, and the Lord guided my tongue when articulating the Edict of Milan."

Constantine sat erect in his gilded chair, proud of his ordained accomplishments and proud to see the adoring eyes of numerous bishops gazing his way, as he continued, "And now the Lord has opened my eyes to see the important role that *you*, my bishops, all play in this grand design. The senseless and unjust persecutions under Diocletian's previous rule had even infuriated many pagans who are now eager to make amends. So, the time is ripe, and if we harvest these raw pagan grapes right now, your churches will surely overflow with your covenant's richly cultivated wine. Know this, if you fail to seize this divine opportunity, which I graciously present to you, it will surely shrivel and rot, leaving you nothing but malodorous compost. So, look beyond your petty self-interests and swing open your doors to an entire empire—an empire awaiting to be harvested!"

The majority of bishops applauded jubilantly, as one after another stood and cheered, "Hail Caesar! Hail Constantine!"

Another bishop yelled to his brethren to squelch their cheers, and as they did, he shouted, "Your words, Caesar, can only proclaim the divine truth! We must enlighten all of Rome about the blood and body of Christ. I propose we adopt the pagans' sacred vestments and miter. These spiritual embellishments have proven quite effective when schooling the masses, and will augment our own positions and powers. After all, *control* is something we all can learn from Rome, and of course *you*, oh mighty Caesar!"

Constantine nodded graciously, as another bishop added, "Much light has shone today, and let us not forget how Jesus has been described by John in his Gospel, as being one with the light, which God created on the first day in Genesis. So, let that light shine upon us all!"

Another bishop rose to his feet clutching onto a staff and interjected, "Yes, my brother, but let us make sure not to reveal the gospels of Thomas or Philip. Their blasphemous scripts proclaim that this light can be found within all of us, for Genesis clearly states that man was made in the image of God. This would allow anyone to find God's light within himself, without our astute guidance. After all, this is what Irenaeus rightfully fought hard to silence over a hundred years ago." Forcefully, he banged his staff on the floor, and beckoned, "It's imperative that we maintain control, to be the ruling shepherds over our capricious flock."

Constantine smiled. "*Control*, yes, excellent! You have clearly grasped my divine vision, and are now on the right road. A road that shall be fashioned of tightly interlocked stones. The results thus far make it clear that our chariot will indeed ride supreme, and Christianity shall prevail. My faith in you was not ill-founded. Please, take it upon yourselves to deliberate at will."

The Catholic bishops cheered and heartily applauded, as Arius and his followers, along with the Donatists, angrily shook their heads and pushed their way toward the exit. One angry Donatist gazed at Constantine, and bitterly griped, "You're nothing but an atheist!"

Constantine's head snapped sideways, as his large piercing eyes zeroed-in on the bishop. "How soon you Christians forget. *We* Romans coined the word 'atheist' to describe *you*! Yes, *you*, who denied the gods. How fast and unwittingly you steal a creation from its master, claim it as your own, and then have the gall to reverse it, so you can lambaste its master. That, in itself, is as lame and ridiculous as your accusation. However, it does underscore what we here have said; namely Christianity has already adopted its rivals' traits, and shall continue to do so!"

The blank expression on the bishop's face, along with those of his Donatist sympathizers, defined befuddlement, as Constantine vehemently barked, "And if you cannot see God's divine hand at work in these proceedings, then perhaps the wrath of God will awaken you!"

At the exit, two seething guards grabbed their gladius swords by the handle. Dutifully they both looked over at Constantine and eagerly awaited his command. Arius and the Donatist bishops suddenly felt the immense weight of the emperor's power bearing down on them, as if the massive Arch of Constantine itself. Nervously, their jittery eyes gazed at one another. Slowly they looked up at Constantine, as a cool chill rippled their skin. Constantine sat outwardly rigid, sequestering the rage streaming through his veins. Calmly, he leaned back. Then matter-of-factly, he waved his hand, thus signaling their release. The disgruntled band of bishops eagerly departed, while some defiantly bellowed and moaned, making their utter dissatisfaction clear to all.

Simultaneously, Alexander and several eminent bishops formed a procession leading toward an enormous table at the rear of the chamber. Others, with large leather satchels on their backs, followed suit. As they plowed their way through, long wooden benches swiveled in their wake, causing a hollow echo to resound throughout the cavernous chamber. The rumbling noise grew even louder as the ecumenical mob encircled the table. From their sacred pouches, they gingerly extracted numerous scrolls, each containing various gospels and texts. The pile mounted, and once complete, looked like a towering pyramid of papyrus, as over eighty codices rounded out the collection.

One elderly bishop slowly weaved his way through the crowd and unsteadily lowered himself onto an ornately carved stool. With a sigh, he rubbed his flaky old dome with one of his gnarled hands. Leaning forward, the wrinkled sage just stared in despair. Then softly his frail voice moaned, "Oh Lord, is this task even possible?"

"Fear not!" a cheerful young bishop retorted. "It doesn't all have to be rewritten, just the ones that are most important."

The wise old bishop turned sharply. With a wrinkled face like a half-rotted old gourd, and the veins in his yellowish eyes bulging, the old man angrily snapped, "And who shall make such a decision?"

The young bishop recoiled as his plump rosy cheeks deflated. As he stood dumbfounded, another bishop quickly retorted, "We can vote on it."

"Fair enough," several others uttered in unison.

A large mass of bishops enthusiastically drew closer to the pile, inciting the old bishop to rise to his rickety feet.

"To hell with you all!" he blasted.

The surrounding bishops just frowned, and then looked over at Alexander. Unperturbed, Alexander looked back down at the table and began sifting through the scrolls.

The old sage snorted and abruptly turned. Angrily, he shuffled his way through the oncoming crowd, which was eager to assist Alexander. Finally reaching the huge wooden doors, he stopped and curiously turned about. To his dismay, not one bishop cared to look in his direction. In humiliation, the old bishop pivoted about and suddenly noticed the two guards. But they, too, didn't even offer a glance, as they simply stood erect and emotionless. Shaking his liver-spotted head, the frail old man turned and gloomily wobbled out of the chamber.

In a mechanical fashion, the guards stepped over and closed the huge wooden doors.

Unaffected, Alexander and the intrepid bishops tackled the monumental task with industrious vigor. For many long hours, they discussed and debated the various principles, rituals, and beliefs, which in some measure reshaped the Christian religion and created what would soon be the official creed.

After several hours, Constantine eagerly walked over to the ecumenical gathering. Sensing the emperor's presence, the bishops turned and looked. With a smile, Constantine waved his hand for them to remain seated. "I am confident that we have made tremendous progress today, yet this shall be only the first of many such meetings. You truly are a noble collaboration. I see Rome's future is in good hands."

One of the bishops energetically rose from the table. "We're eternally grateful, Caesar. You have shown us the light, much like Sol Invictus, whom I know you still adore. In your honor, I shall use the Sun disc as a divine symbol that will adorn all paintings and statuary in my church. It will shed a magnificent radiance over the heads of our Lord, the apostles, and you—*Constantine the Great.*"

Many other bishops rose and fervently avowed to do the same.

"Thank you all," Constantine replied. "I'm especially in union that this corona will not be an offensive mortal crown, but a divine halo. Yes, the Lord does shine, as do his chosen vessels. In gratitude, I shall likewise pass a decree whereby existing temples can be stripped of bronze and other materials that you feel are necessary to accomplish these most sacred tasks." As the bishops enthusiastically applauded, Constantine smiled, and continued, "May all future council meetings be as productive as today's. However, before we part, I must inform you of two new rulings that I have just conceived during your long deliberations. First, in respect to the Bible's reference in Genesis that the world was created in seven days, I shall convert our current eight-day week to seven."

The council looked at one another and unanimously applauded.

With a gracious smile, Constantine motioned for silence. "Second, I am fully aware that Saturday is your holy day of worship, but for the sake of Roman tradition, and universal harmony, it shall now be on the day of Rome's Sun god, Sol Invictus. On the venerable day of the Sun may all Roman Catholics rest and all workshops be closed. Sunday shall now and forever be our holy day of obligation."

The bishops' faces turned pale, as they nervously turned to Alexander. Constantine's contentious ruling put them in an uncomfortable position. Being diehards of ancient Judaic law, apprehension filled their hearts, particularly since Genesis stated that God himself declared Saturday as the day of rest.

One bishop nervously cupped his hand around the side of his mouth, and whispered, "Well, at least that coincides with Christ's resurrection."

They all gingerly nodded, as Alexander briskly turned, and replied, "Very well, Caesar. Sunday it is!"

And thus concluded the first Nicaean Council, one of several, which imprinted a new set of dogmatic tenets that would define critical aspects of Christianity that held fast for many centuries to this very day.

Although a full transcript of this historic meeting does not exist, what the council eventually produced and inaugurated has been recorded. Additionally, many of the rejected scriptures of the rivaling sects have survived; as such, this council quite possibly contained speeches offering similar viewpoints. For added authenticity, direct quotes made by Constantine at this meeting, and at other times, were incorporated to reflect his intentions, as well as what he actually imparted to the bishops. This includes the initial opening remark and his provocative reprimand:

"Even the barbarians now through me, the true servant of God, know God and have learned to reverence him, while you bishops do nothing but that which encourages discord and hatred, and, to speak frankly, which leads to the destruction of the human race."

Constantine's Ecumenical Council was a momentous milestone in Western history. It profoundly organized a diverse group of Christianities into a new and unified entity. Since Jesus' death, three hundred years earlier, these factions were a hodgepodge of obstinate clerics with their own version of the Jesus message. In addition, even though Irenaeus collated the synoptic gospels, which would remain Christendom's official canon, they were not fully embraced by all sects, and this caused intense conflict. For that reason, Constantine decided to intervene. As a result, he forced these intractable bishops to sit face to face under his mediating eye.

Constantine remained fixed on his objectives and continued to arbitrate internal woes, though not always successfully. However, some historians question the effectiveness of Constantine's council for not rectifying some of the disputes. They also cite that the following decade was unstable due to Constantine at first excommunicating Arius and then after continued hostilities, reinstating him. Likewise, there were several other prominent bishops at the council who were ousted in due time. However, these setbacks were understandable and to be expected considering the profound changes being demanded. Even though Constantine was unsure about Arius, and oscillated in his rulings, one must contemplate the end result.

The concept of Jesus being the subordinate earthly Son of the supreme and heavenly God the Father was not just the opinion of Arius and his clan; it was a widespread belief held by many Christians for three hundred years. Many scriptures, both in and out of the canon, mention Jesus as being subordinate to his Father, however, after Constantine's council, this Arian viewpoint was forever quashed. Hence, Constantine's objective, regardless of oscillations and unrest, ultimately prevailed.

Furthermore, Constantine's ecumenical precedent, whereby emperors chaired these religious councils, continued for another five hundred years. This continued right up to the creation of the official seat of pope. Most importantly, many noteworthy rulings at Constantine's first council did stay intact, regardless of these disputes. This becomes very clear once we review some of the colossal rulings made at the Nicaean Council and beyond, which unequivocally achieved Constantine's desired result.

Aside from the ecumenical councils, Constantine passed earth-shattering legislation. This was evident when the headstrong Donatists refused to comply; Constantine ordered them to surrender their churches to the Catholics, while also confiscating their smaller meeting places. Moreover, when noncompliant sects refused to evacuate a church or facility, Constantine did not refrain from using the military to physically implement evictions. Many other legal programs directly empowered Catholic bishops, so that from the first council onward, Christianity would have the exclusive political support of the Roman Empire, support that it utilized to the fullest and for many centuries.

Moreover, one cannot overlook the profound and indelible changes that Constantine's Nicaean Council made. On that day, the profession of faith was born, which after centuries of discord finally described God as homoousios and unquestionably divine, consisting of three natures: the Father, Son, and Holy Ghost. This was not only the first appearance of the word homoousios in Christian scriptures, but this word, which Constantine demanded be included, had actually been banned by Church leaders as heretical only forty years before. Therefore, it was largely due to Constantine that Jesus would eternally be described as "of one substance."

Adding further to this decree was the term that Jesus was begotten not made. This put an end to the centuries long debate over whether there was a time that Jesus did not exist. That he was begotten of the Father indicated that he existed before his earthly appearance, and this was vital to ensuring his divinity.

In addition, Constantine's Nicene Creed created the phrase, "God from God, Light from Light, true God from true God", which is still incanted in every Roman Catholic Church to this day. Additionally, this council inaugurated the Catholic Church's daily repeated phrase, and firm belief in "one holy, Catholic, and apostolic church."

These were all profound doctrines of Christian ideology and of church identity. That the Roman Catholic Church was now a monolithic enterprise was beyond being important for the religion—it would be colossally instrumental in shaping the future world. And a prime mover in making that become manifest was the Roman emperor Constantine.

DANTE: *A Spark amid Darkness*

A relentless breeze rippled over the banks of the Ronco River and throughout Ravenna. Seated at his ornately carved wooden desk, Dante Alighieri could hear the rustling of trees outside his window. He had put the final touches on his *Divina Commedia* only weeks before and was now preparing to depart for Bologna. He had recently received an invitation from Giovanni del Virgilio, Latin professor at Bologna's prestigious university.

Dante penned some last-minute thoughts about a current poem, then placed his quill down on his desk, content to have harvested the ripe fruits of inspiration before they withered and died. Meticulously, he then collated the parchments and placed them in perfect parallel to his Bible

Pivoting about, Dante grasped his polished, jasper rosary beads and gazed down at them. A warm smile etched his chiseled features. The beads had belonged to his beloved mother who died when he was only six. Reverently, Dante kissed them twice, then gently hung them on a brass, angel wall-hook.

He wrapped his red *lucco* around his shoulders, pulled the tie strings, and wove a neat knot. He grasped his small leather satchel, then turned to inspect the room one last time. He huffed. The bronze crucifix on the wall was slightly crooked. It always seemed to go off-kilter when the door slammed. Dante leveled it, crossed himself, and exited.

The four-horse carriage arrived on schedule, as the coachman pulled back the reins and came to a stop. Dante climbed aboard and nestled himself in, anticipating the long and bumpy journey that lie ahead. The coachman then cracked his whip, nipping the lead horse's hefty rear. With a snort and a jerk, the horse bucked and started his team racing forward.

Riding over rugged Tuscan mountains and lush cultivated valleys, rich with vibrant vineyards and healthy baaing goats, the hours peacefully rolled by like the passing scenery. Dante was deeply engrossed in jotting down some ethereal thoughts when suddenly he felt the horses slow down to a jolting trot. With his curiosity piqued, Dante could hear the coachman as he mumbled and coughed. It was then that Dante caught a glimpse of a small village outside his open window. Without warning, a horrific stench swiftly saturated Dante's cabin. Frantically, he grasped his handkerchief and covered his large aquiline nose and thin lips.

Dante thrust his head out the cabin window; his stomach violently flipping topsy-turvy, as vomit surged up into his mouth and then repulsively subsided. The corrosive coating of bile made Dante gag, as the acidic liquid began to burn his throat. Helplessly, Dante gazed upon hundreds of dead bodies all ravaged by the plague. Raw and maligned carcasses, covered with dark boils and pus, were piled up near the roadside like diseased animals, while the air reeked of effluvia.

Priests and townspeople, wearing handkerchief masks, stained gloves, and draped in long garments, worked side-by-side trying desperately to stack the rotting corpses that had accumulated at an alarming rate. Huge pyres roared in the distance, as the despondent survivors tried to keep pace with the rapid number of cremations. Pungent smells of wormwood, sulfur, and juniper burned in the villagers' hearths; all just vain attempts to eradicate the asphyxiating smell of the Black Death. The potent odors, however, only added to Dante's nausea.

As the carriage came alongside an industrious priest, who wore a linen cloth around his face while he prepared the bodies for cremation, Dante called out to his driver to stop. As the coach slowed down, Dante leaned out the window and offered to lend a hand, but the overwhelmed priest turned and waved for him to move on. When Dante inquired a second time, the priest pulled down his face covering and offered the poet thanks, but informed him of the quarantine. Reaffixing his mask, the priest dutifully returned to the onerous task of cremating the dead and offering solace to survivors.

Overcome by the horrific visions, Dante pulled his head back in, as the coachman eagerly snapped the reins. Closing his window, Dante removed the handkerchief from his face and feverishly tried to create saliva to quench his burning esophagus. In utter disbelief, he watched as the decaying village slowly scrolled by his window, like a satanic slideshow. Filled with sorrow, Dante's heart and soul burned, like his bile-scorched throat.

After several dark moments, in a place out of time, the distressing scenes of horror slowly receded from sight. Dante's face was purple, as he flung open his cabin window and gasped desperately for air. Looking back, with tears filling his reddened eyes, Dante pensively reflected on the apt words he had penned in the *Inferno*, "... I crossed over and began to mount that little known and lightless road to ascend into the shining world again."

Alas, Dante had just witnessed hell on Earth. But now, as the abominable vision finally vanished, his eyes gazed upon lush greenery and a distant lake. With content, Dante recalled:

"Sweet azure of the sapphire of the east,
was gathering on the serene horizon,
its pure and perfect radiance, a feast."

With a clear vista now before him, a gratifying calm befell Dante, as the carriage continued its journey. The pleasant sounds of frolicking chickens and lambs, and even the fertilizing scent of cow manure, offered welcome signs of life, as he once again jotted down some reflective thoughts.

The sun had moved another five degrees, when Dante's coach finally entered the bustling city of Bologna. Passing Roman-styled arcades and buildings, all fashioned out of Bologna's pinkish sandstone, Dante recalled his first visit, which had developed into a two-year stint several years earlier. As the carriage made its way toward the university, Dante spotted a tall lanky lad, waving enthusiastically.

The horses let out an irritable grunt, as their mouth-bits drew back and rattled their teeth. The coachman yanked the reins a second time to ensure they heeded his command. As the carriage came to a rocking stop, Dante could hear the horses' hooves clattering as they anxiously stepped in place.

The attentive youngster, wearing brown pantaloons and a billowy white shirt with ruffled sleeves, ran over and swung open the carriage door.

"*Signore* Dante, *saluti!* Please, follow me."

"*Saluti,*" Dante echoed, as the young lad scurried toward the entrance.

As Dante followed, his eyes gazed up at the façade, then down at the carved doorway that he knew so well. Passing over the threshold, they entered into the university's refined lobby.

As Dante trailed the silent youth, he gazed up again to admire the huge barrel-vaulted ceilings and the fluted pilasters with Corinthian capitals that lined the corridors. Large tapestries commemorating the Crusades decorated the endless expanse of walls, firing Dante's memories of his great-great-grandfather, Cacciaguida, who had fought to regain the Holy Land from the Muslims, yet in vain, becoming a famous martyr.

They entered the Latin Arts wing, then turned down a small corridor, one unfamiliar to Dante. Finally, they arrived at an arched wooden doorway. The gangly lad flipped the metal latch and pushed open the door. He then extended his arm, motioning Dante to enter. *"Continui!"*

Dante crossed the threshold, and abruptly found himself face-to-face with a short burly man, who bellowed, *"Infine!* I get to meet Dante Alighieri. The soon to be slayer—or is it pioneer—of verse?"

A bit startled, Dante stepped back, and replied, "Uh...a pioneer, *naturalmente*...and, I assume you are?"

Sensing his error in etiquette, the burly man replied, *"Scusilo.* My enthusiasm trampled my manners. I am Giovanni del Virgilio. As my invitation stated, I am the professor of Latin Arts here at Bologna. *Signore* Dante, I am intrigued by your work."

Dante smiled cautiously. *"Incuriosito,* you say. Yet you question my ability, as well as my intentions?"

"Signore Dante, you have made bold maneuvers on several fronts with your *Inferno* and *Purgatorio* cantos. First, you abandon Latin and use our common Italian vernacular. Second, you invent a new *terza rima* to construct the work. And third, *Signore* Dante, you make religious judgments and enforce the Lord's will in an allegory of your own devising.

These are quite serious and lofty grounds upon which you tread."

"Serious grounds for a serious topic, Giovanni. My allegory has many religious sources of inspiration for my grand concept, but the judgments are not mine. Nay, for they follow the Lord's master plan. A plan that we mortals all must abide or suffer the consequences. I have just witnessed such divine wrath on my journey here today, for can any soul truly escape the authority of God, or the plague's deadly omen?"

Giovanni nodded amicably, as Dante proceeded, "As for my penchant for poetic invention, it comes naturally to any inspired mind that realizes that new revelations require new forms to express them. Our age is slowly reawakening to the significance of numbers and how they construct God's divine plan; therefore, triple rhyme was mandatory to express not merely my plan, Professor del Virgilio, but His plan."

Dante stepped over and placed his leather satchel on the professor's desk, as he continued, "Moreover, you inquire as to why I chose the Italian language, and I say, it is because I believe that it sings to our blood brothers in the most succinct fashion. Homer wrote in Greek, Virgil in Latin, hence I must write in Italian. As you may know, I have spent much time scrutinizing the many Italian dialects throughout the land in an attempt to secure the most suitable for all Italians to embrace. I have even bestowed higher praise upon your Bolognese dialect over my own Florentine tongue. However, Saint Francis of Assisi was actually the first to attempt this, for he wrote his song *Canticle of the Sun* in Italian. And I, too, have found the Italian tongue most pleasing and most fitting for my work, for the beauty of its tone only adds to its allure."

Giovanni had been standing fixed and pensive, but now spontaneously retorted, "I would still prefer to see your profound words in Latin, Dante, for all great texts at the university are in the tongue of our Roman ancestors, the language of scholars."

The professor pivoted and grasped a codex from his large bookshelf, which spanned an entire wall, and said, "Even lost ancient Greek texts, most of which were recently translated into Latin, demand that Latin remain the sole salvation of erudite men." Placing the codex back into its slot, he added, "Moreover, as you mentioned, the Italian language is indeed plagued by many dialects. Even here in Bologna, the intellectual epicenter of the city flows with our cultured tongue, while a mere walk to the humble outskirts reveals a vulgar variant. But don't be deceived, Dante. Under my veil of misgivings, I am quite confident that your words shall always find an audience, for you are surely marked for greatness. The intensity, purpose, and divine order of your cantos are without equal. Pure genius. I just pray that a final *Paradiso* section will follow someday."

"*Logicamente*, it must follow, and it did! Fear not, Professor, for I have it with me."

Giovanni recoiled, as Dante pulled the manuscript out of his leather case. With a sanguine smile, Dante placed the heavenly conclusion of his divine efforts in the professor's anxious hands.

Giovanni looked down in awe as he blurted, "*Fantastico!*"

The professor's eyes reverently gazed at the thick stack of parchments, while his right hand gently caressed the top page. "I can't wait to peruse your grand finale!" Gazing up, he continued, "But, Dante, I have delayed long enough. I must tell you the chief reason for your invitation. It is my sincere pleasure to bestow upon you Bologna's famous laurel crown."

Dante swallowed hard and struggled to maintain his smile, but couldn't. "Professor, I sincerely thank you and

Bologna for that wonderful honor, but I am compelled to hold true to my convictions. It is a personal necessity that I receive the crown from my home, Florence, and from her alone."

Giovanni's enthusiasm died. "Dante, you still suffer from the harsh exile sentenced upon you by the pope and his Black Guelph faction so many years ago. Florence, that most beautiful flower, is no longer what she used to be, so why cling to her fallen petals?"

Dante looked up with solemn eyes. "For one simple reason. Love. Love is that mystical force that drives some men to greed and others to greatness. I have endured great agony at the hands of sinful and corrupt men, both in political and papal office, who moreover lack any sense of morals. There is little that grieves me more than seeing inept and avaricious politicians poison the beautiful flower that once was my home. But I will never abandon my firm beliefs—beliefs that saturate my soul and dictate my destiny." Dante's voice rose with ardent passion, as he continued, "I shall be the Lord's torch, and shall convey in a new and vivid form of verse His divine light, to illuminate our century, which languishes in darkness, with the intent of inspiring souls among us and those henceforth through the ages to cultivate a more benevolent and brighter future, one that will burn with fervent intensity!"

Giovanni smiled. "Well, if anyone can accomplish such a great feat, *signore* Dante, it most certainly is you!"

❊   ❊   ❊

Dante had in fact been invited to Bologna by Giovanni del Virgilio to receive the city's highest honor, and had briefly stayed in Bologna previously. Although the dialogue in this vignette was created, Dante's disenchantment was real and recorded in many ways. The decay of morals, and increase of greed and lust for power, by both secular and religious factions, all plagued Dante's intellectual mind and religious soul. His own wrongful banishment for graft by Pope Boniface VIII added heavily to this humiliation.

The Black and White Guelphs divided Dante's beloved city of Florence, causing much havoc. The Black faction had supported Pope Boniface VIII—not one of the Vatican's star assets. The pope's lust for complete spiritual and temporal control was clearly reflected in his own words, when he declared, "It is necessary for salvation that every living creature be under submission to the Roman pontiff." Thus began the pope's struggle for ultimate political and religious power as he locked horns with the Germanic rulers of the Holy Roman Empire.

Dante viewed this collective degeneration as a downward fall from grace. Being exiled from Florence, never to return or see his wife again, may have made Dante's soul vacant, but the Lord filled that void and propelled his pen to the summit of world literature. Five hundred and eight years after his death, the city of Florence regretted erasing the memory of Dante from his hometown, and they erected an impressive tomb for the famous poet inside the Cathedral of Santa Croce. Yet Dante's body, to this day, remains far from Florence in the city of Ravenna.

Dante Alighieri was not only the most brilliant writer of his age—and one of mankind's greatest bards, on par with Shakespeare and Homer—but his immense influence has cascaded down the centuries to inspire countless authors, artists, composers, and politicians to enhance civilization.

Among others are the composers Franz Liszt and Peter Tchaikovsky, artists Gustav Doré, Botticelli, Rodin, and William Blake, the writer Henry Wadsworth Longfellow, and more recently, this author, with the historical thriller *Liszt's Dante Symphony*, and Dan Brown, whose recent novel

Inferno was made into a feature film. And in small measure, this quasi-fictional narrative once again attempts to illuminate the light that was Dante—a spark amid darkness.

BRUNELLESCHI: *Master Builder*

Born in Florence in 1377, Filippo Brunelleschi was well known by all Florentines, for he had invented the mathematical laws of linear perspective that the ancient Romans apparently exercised, yet were lost to time. Brunelleschi's geometric invention gave a whole new generation of artists and architects the primary tool to develop earth-shattering wonders in paint, like those created by Verrocchio, Leonardo, Michelangelo, and countless others, not to mention 3D architectural plans.

However, Brunelleschi was also remembered in Florence for losing the bronze door competition to his rival Lorenzo Ghiberti. Ghiberti's magnificently sculpted doors adorned the Baptistery and immediately enthralled the entire city. In turn, Ghiberti was garnished with the utmost adoration and world fame. In humiliation, Filippo left Florence, only to return many years later when a golden opportunity presented itself—the new dome competition.

Finally, here was Brunelleschi's chance to regain his stolen title, and the respect he knew he deserved. The design was for the city's huge Santa Maria del Fiore cathedral. Originally designed in 1296, the huge project lingered for over a century, facing revisions and cutbacks. By 1419, the building had finally reached near completion, except for the massive void at the top, which somehow was to be capped off with a dome.

Brunelleschi was dismayed to learn that his old rival, Ghiberti, also entered the competition, but more problematic, however, was that the project posed an additional conundrum. The dome's drum foundation was not round like the Pantheon, but octagonal. This was an engineering first, which entered the participants into new and uncharted territory. Brunelleschi had previously traveled to Rome and meticulously studied the Pantheon. Despite the obvious differences, Brunelleschi had deciphered many of the hidden tricks and traits of the Pantheon's unique anatomy. Confident that this covert acquisition gave him the edge over his archrival, Ghiberti, and every other contender, Brunelleschi feverishly set to work on his own master plan.

When the day finally arrived, the hopefuls submitted their grand plans. As the judging committee sifted through the entries, their jaws suddenly dropped when they gazed at Brunelleschi's radical plans. For not only was his design astoundingly unique, but Filippo had the audacity, or sheer incompetency, to do away with the use of wooden centering.

Centering had long been the established and mandatory approach for erecting arches. It entailed creating huge wooden arches whereby masons would lay and set their bricks on top, thus following the curved wooden form. When some of the other contestants heard that Filippo was abandoning this only known procedure, they duly ridiculed him. Meanwhile, others anticipated new solutions.

It was clear, the octagonal obstacle, along with its unprecedented height, demanded a new approach. At first skeptical, the committee slowly recognized the validity of Filippo's engineering skills when his flawless miniature model awed the public audience. Brunelleschi had even penciled out plans for constructing his own proprietary cranes, jacks, and scaffolding to complete the daunting task, all without the use of centering. No detail was left out, for nothing had escaped Filippo's discerning eye.

With the backing of the highly influential Medici banking family, the committee initially commissioned Brunelleschi to construct a smaller dome in the city to test his theories in practice. It was soon evident that Filippo was the engineering savant that Florence had long prayed for, and to his everlasting delight, Brunelleschi won the contract.

Filippo engaged the project with fervor, and cautiously supervised every facet of the operation. The master builder even constructed his new-fangled hoists and machinery in addition to safety mechanisms that saved many lives. Years later, these devices would intrigue the young Leonardo, and deeply influenced his own array of mechanical creations. Ingenuity begets influence, influence begets inspiration, and inspiration begets ingenuity—a perfect circle.

But Brunelleschi was in for some aggravation. A few judges on the advisory panel were still skeptical of his abilities, and they insultingly appointed his rival, Ghiberti, to become the project's supervisor. Resolved to never fall in Ghiberti's shadow again, Brunelleschi soon made it abundantly clear that *he*, not Ghiberti, was the grand master. As engineering obstacles arose, Ghiberti stood mute. The complex project was far out his creative or technical reach, thus proving that Brunelleschi alone possessed not only all the concepts but also all the solutions. Filippo's solutions single-handedly escalated engineering, architecture, and the art of dome construction to new heights.

Brunelleschi's miraculous dome even inaugurated the first double-dome construction in history, which even facilitated a staircase sandwiched in-between. Located inside one of the vertical ribs, it was conveniently used to ascend to the apex of the cupola. In total, these radical features had not only initially perplexed the judging committee but also made Brunelleschi's design seem ridiculously unfeasible.

Therefore, on the heavily anticipated day of the dome's completion, the architect was presented with a double reward; for his biting critics fell into an eerie silence, while the rest of the city showered him with praise and glory. Brunelleschi's masterwork broke many astounding records, and rightfully boosted Filippo into the stratosphere of world fame. Not only was Filippo's design an instant success, but his double-domed blueprint would even be adopted by Michelangelo and Dela Porta many years later when they designed Saint Peter's dome. Thus, with Brunelleschi's new masterpiece, Florence became the technological focal point and crown jewel of the budding Renaissance.

This aptly brings us to the following chain of events, which also validates how the influence of artistic genius spurs others to greatness.

In 1475, Brunelleschi's friend, Paolo Toscanelli, was enamored by Filippo's new architectural wonder. Paolo was a brilliant physician and astronomer, who had even taught Filippo geometry. Toscanelli was anxious to conduct celestial experiments atop the soaring lantern (which was designed and mounted by Verrocchio) that crowned the new dome. With the committee's consent, Paolo rigged up a plate with a small aperture at the base of the lantern; this allowed sunlight to pass down the drum directly to the distant floor below. In essence, Paolo created a highly accurate sundial, and this allowed him to make precise mathematical corrections to the prevailing calculations that charted the sun's movements. This led Toscanelli to calculate the vernal equinox and summer solstice with complete accuracy, and also to devise a new and superior form of navigation.

The existing methods of navigation, whereby navigators used maps with astrolabes to calculate their position by tracking the Pole Star, had reached a dead end. It worked in the Mediterranean Sea, but as mariners traveled south, they realized the Pole Star's position lowered on the horizon, thus becoming insufficient for global navigation. Toscanelli realized that the sun was the best source for global navigation, and with his superior maps, which were rendered years earlier in 1459 (quite possibly by his friend Leonardo da Vinci), Toscanelli was the first person in his age to put forth the idea of sailing west to reach India.

Six years before in 1453, the Turks had conquered Byzantium. That conquest severed land travel for Europeans attempting to reach the Far East. As such, another route became a necessity. Hence, Toscanelli was extremely eager to make his theory known as a viable solution.

Toscanelli promptly appealed to his friend, Fernão Martines, who worked at the court of King Afonso in Portugal, for Paolo was well aware of their great strides in vessel construction and exploration. However, Paolo's new plan fell upon deaf ears. Seven long years passed before a zealous relative of Martines' finally contacted Toscanelli. That man happened to be the gutsy navigator from Genoa, Christopher Columbus.

COLUMBUS: *Courageous & Unjustly Maligned Explorer*

Christopher Columbus was intrigued by Paolo Toscanelli's maps and bold route plan, and as such, eagerly tested the waters further south off the coast of Africa, near the Canary Islands. Finding that the currents appeared more favorable, he quickly adopted Toscanelli's plan.

As an additional reinforcement, Columbus was also aware of the provocative theory by Augustus' tutor Posidonius, fourteen hundred years previously, who also believed that the Indies could be reached by sailing westward. Hence, with Toscanelli's recent studies adding mathematical validity to this intriguing proposition, Columbus fervently pushed forward to secure a sponsor for his daring expedition.

Unfortunately, like Toscanelli, Columbus also hit a dead end with the Portuguese, thus prompting his appeal to King Ferdinand and Queen Isabella of Spain. It would take almost a decade before the Italian navigator won their patronage, for the monarchs had been heavily preoccupied with other affairs.

As it happened, King Ferdinand was in the process of sterilizing Spain of all infidels of the Christian faith, and his pogrom began with the expulsion of Muslims. However, the cost of the long purge seriously drained the imperial coffers. A new source of revenue was mandatory and Columbus' proposition sounded rather enticing, as the promise of rich spices, textiles, and gold from Asia seemed the ideal remedy to the Spanish Crown's immense debt.

Marco Polo's famous journey and enlightening book, *Il Millione*, had previously opened up the Orient to Europeans in 1298. However, in 1453, Sultan Mehmet II sacked Constantinople, whereby severing the land route. Now, thirty-nine years later, Ferdinand and the pope shared the fear of Muslim expansion. Therefore, the notion of spreading and strengthening Christianity also added a vital incentive. As such, the Spanish monarchs had no choice but to authorize the bold exploratory mission, and as we know, Columbus courageously sailed into history.

The year 1492 indelibly marked that historic voyage, which became a colossal milestone in human history. It cannot be understated that Columbus' tenacity and unrelenting resolve opened the new door to an entire hemisphere, doubling trade and spreading Christian influence across the globe. Furthermore, even though most educated men knew that the world was round, navigation of the vast expanse of the Atlantic had never been attempted in the bold fashion that Columbus mapped out. Up to that time, all European navigators were trained to hug the coastline, and only rarely ventured out to the precarious point of losing sight of land. When they did, their journeys were for a maximum of seven to eight days. Meanwhile, Columbus took his men out into a vast and uncharted ocean for two terrifying months.

That feat alone displayed Columbus' courage and determination; however, it also revealed the immense belief in his abilities, for his men put their lives in his hands, while abandoning safety and civilization, to challenge the unknown. This is crucial to understanding Columbus, who in recent years has been maligned for, among other things, being a cruel administrator. This indictment shall be challenged in due course. Most are familiar with Columbus' famous discovery in 1492, but not with his other exploits or how unanticipated events hurled Columbus into a deadly tempest of ravaging seas and personal ruinous slander.

Columbus journeyed to the New World four times, yet before his last voyage, the Italian navigator had lost favor with his Spanish patrons. This was due to his failure to generate enough profits for the Spanish monarchs and his poor management of the newly formed colonies that he established in the West Indies. Columbus rightfully argued that they expected him to govern over a wild tropical island, inhabited by naked natives, as if it were a cultivated Spanish city. Hispaniola (present day Haiti and the Dominican Republic) was a large island in the Caribbean that Columbus discovered, and where he was later asked to establish his primary colony. Unfortunately, many factors had quickly aligned that turned Columbus' governorship and his life into a disaster. To better understand his misfortune, we need to backtrack to his first voyage.

Upon discovering Hispaniola, Columbus encountered the Arawak natives, whose chief was Guacanagari. Four supreme kings ruled the island and the natives told Columbus of the cannibalistic Carib tribe that stole and raped their women while ferociously eating men and children. Soon after, fifty-five Caribs attacked seven of Columbus' men, but the Spaniards' weapons scared them off, thus proving to the Arawaks their superior might. Meanwhile, Columbus ordered the shipwrecked Santa

Maria to be used to build a fort (naming the site La Navidad), and had a small garrison of thirty-nine officers remain with the friendly Arawaks. Meanwhile Columbus returned to Spain to break the astounding news.

The king and queen were enamored by stories of exotic tropical islands inhabited by naked natives, but mostly by the prospects of gold and other riches. Columbus was outfitted with seventeen ships and was sent on his second return voyage; this time, however, with the added responsibility of establishing a fully functional colony, and being the governor of Hispaniola. Despondent over his new political assignment, Columbus was yet to face the real catastrophe that was to await him when he returned to the picturesque island. To his utter horror, all his officers had been brutally massacred and their fort burnt to the ground.

Guacanagari had been injured and claimed that two rival kings, Caonabo and Behechio, had attacked his village and killed the Spaniards. Their alleged motives were that the Spaniards had taken their women (possibly to reclaim those abducted by Caonabo) and disease. However, the Spaniards' belongings were found in the friendly natives' huts. Equally suspicious, Guacanagari's injury, once revealed, showed no visible wounds. The mysterious massacre was a bloody omen of worse things to befall Columbus.

Therefore, right from the fatal start, Columbus faced a dangerous uphill battle. Making a new settlement further east, Columbus and his crew of fifteen hundred established the town of Isabela. Only this time the natives would be handled more cautiously—some were converted to Christians and others enslaved. While the slaves and colonists panned for gold, Columbus and his brother amassed two hundred men and hunted down Caonabo. Upon his capture, the hostile king confessed to killing twenty Spaniards at La Navidad, and worse yet, admitted to being friendly to the new wave of Spaniards in order to replicate the first massacre. Rather than kill Caonabo, Columbus imprisoned him for deportation to Spain. The victory ensured peace on Hispaniola for a year.

Nevertheless, with the governor spending most of his time exploring the Caribbean, slanderous rumors arose. Evidently, the Spanish settlers from the second voyage were all greedy vagabonds that only sought the riches of gold. Like the Dominican priest, Bartolomé de Las Casas, said, these unscrupulous souls expected to find gold in abundance and sitting readily available for the taking. The prospect that to find gold required digging, sifting or mining caused these lazy Spaniards to mistreat the natives by working them harder while also drifting from location to location in their frenzied quest. King Ferdinand and Columbus had expected these people to be true settlers, thus building homes and churches and nurturing families. Instead, their licentious and selfish ways only incensed the natives and caused Columbus undue anguish, as they blamed Columbus for their financial misfortunes.

This growing rebellion prompted Columbus to return to Spain, along with Caonabo in chains, to update the sovereigns. Before departing, Columbus appointed Francisco Roldan as mayor to rule in his absence. However, Bishop Fonseca detained Columbus for two humiliating years in Spain; while back on Hispaniola, order quickly degenerated into chaos. Dissension ran wild and reprisals grew wicked. Both natives and Spaniards who committed crimes were recklessly sentenced, jailed, tortured, or hung. When Columbus finally returned on his third voyage, he faced an unruly mass of rebels reveling in anarchy.

This chapter of Columbus' career has caused the most outrage and vilification. Previous to his governorship, Columbus generated deep loyalty and admiration. However, the ugly situation on Hispaniola is the root cause for modern analysts to besmirch Columbus. However, the evidence largely points to others as being the villains, such as the traitorous mayor Roldan, who wreaked havoc in Columbus' absence, the whimpering Spaniards that blamed Columbus for their financial woes, and other factors that need to be woven into the Columbus story.

As we know, men of the past cannot be judged by modern American standards. Despite the centuries that separate us from Columbus, we can actually find third world nations today with similar sensibilities as Columbus' fifteenth century Spain, and we can also find primitive tribes located in remote corners of the world that mirror the sensibilities of the natives that Columbus faced. Therefore, because our cultivated society is the result of countless centuries of refinement and progress we cannot expect third world nations today to miraculously behave like Americans, nor can we expect archaic tribesmen today to be more than what they are.

That said, some records indicate that Columbus engaged in cruel practices while reprimanding rebels on Hispaniola. This resulted in cutting off men's ears or slicing their lips. Naturally, this makes any modern American cringe, and it instantly elicits condemnation. Although we rightfully would never tolerate this today, we need to ask what the standard practices of Spanish law were. For that matter, what were the practices of many other nations throughout the fifteenth century? We have all heard of the hostile treatment of even petty criminals having their hands chopped off for theft, nonbelievers burned at the stake, or even the brutal practice of pouring molten metal down a traitor's throat. So were the brutalities on Hispaniola so extraordinary? It certainly appears not, especially when we take this a step further.

Was it Columbus, or his administrative officers who committed these acts? Records indicate that Alonso de Hojeda cut off a deceitful chief's ear, not Columbus. And how innocent were the rebels? We also know that Columbus spent very little time on Hispaniola. His digest and charts detail his many discoveries of various islands in the West Indies, and we know he loathed the position of governor. Naturally, his being the governor makes him responsible for his men's actions, which included his brother Bartolomé, and in that regard, we can administer varying degrees of dissatisfaction or blame. Since he was a man of his times, we can also ask what exactly did his superiors in Spain do? Were they ethically above this sort of treatment? We know Columbus was reprimanded, shackled in chains, and then shipped back to Spain for questioning. But we need to probe the royal actions further.

King Ferdinand was furious that his new colony was in disarray, as law and order was mandatory for maintaining productivity. We must have no illusions—productivity was first and foremost for the crown and filling Ferdinand's empty coffers. Ferdinand was obliged to take swift action to pacify the humiliated settlers and natives, especially those that were innocent: after all, these abuses were occurring a vast ocean away from their king and under the administration of a partially absentee governor. The devastating massacre of the first colonists and news of the cannibalistic Caribs were also constant reminders of this raw and untamed world, and with communications alone taking a month or more to arrive, Ferdinand could have received word that his entire expedition and colony was annihilated months after the fact. His investment needed to be protected, so a stern reprimand was indeed in order.

This brings us to the all-important issue of comparing the Italian governor to his Spanish king in the matter of meting out punishment. Evidence indicates that Columbus was stern but judicious. The earless chief, that Hojeda hacked, pleaded for forgiveness and Columbus pardoned him. Rebels who threatened the very survival of Hispaniola were indeed punished; yet, most often, Columbus tried to prevent his men from committing sinful acts. In fact, on his previous return voyage to Spain, Columbus had to prevent his men from throwing the natives overboard. They were driven off course and food supplies were scarce, hence the Spaniards wished to eliminate some of the competition for rations by killing the natives. Fortunately, Columbus' lecture about Christian compassion prevailed.

Furthermore, the naïve comments made many years later by Las Casas that fueled modern historians to alter the Columbus story must be addressed. The Spanish priest certainly made valid criticisms regarding the cruel mistreatment of natives that are deplorable and regrettable. However, the mayhem that grew was certainly not Columbus' intentions, and this malevolence grew while he was busy exploring or building the new town of Isabela. Working the natives to pan for gold was prompted by Columbus' dire need to accrue gold, not for himself, but for Ferdinand. For to return to Spain empty handed would have certainly eliminated funding and terminated the New World project.

Moreover, as time passed, Las Casas had become unwittingly biased. He tells of two million natives being so overworked that their numbers dropped to two thousand. These massive amounts of deaths we now know were largely due to the invisible diseases that the Europeans innocently brought with them, not cruelty. This epidemic, mistaken as genocide, caused Las Casas to piously say "The Indians were not so much guilty of one single mortal sin." Moreover, he blamed Columbus for calling the natives hostile. Evidently, Las Casas somehow forgot how the thirty-nine Spaniards at La Navidad were slaughtered, or how Columbus personally encountered many native tribes that attacked his crew without provocation and clearly with hostile intentions. Therefore, Columbus had far more on his plate than most then and today realized.

In stark contrast, King Ferdinand and Queen Isabella were steering Spain into its most ugly period by initiating ferocious pogroms. They had just finished the first phase of the operation by expelling the Muslims and would now commence on the most brutal initiative, the Spanish Inquisition.

With the aid of their second in command, Bishop Fonseca, the royal couple began to purge Spain of all its Jewish inhabitants, as well as forcing all nonbelievers to convert to Catholicism or join the thousands of others who were set ablaze as human torches, or had their skin removed with hot pincers. The enormous barbarism that ensued under Ferdinand's reign was monstrously wicked. There is controversy over the total death toll, with numbers ranging from 10,000 to 150,000, but regardless of the actual number, King Ferdinand was a mass murderer. But this is never mentioned by modern historians who hastily criticize and dishonor Columbus for being a cruel governor. Columbus certainly was deficient in his political duties and could have performed a better job, yet in comparison to King Ferdinand, Columbus was far more humane and just. Furthermore, Columbus was unfortunately the subservient pawn of a duplicitous king.

Most revealing, is that King Ferdinand dropped the charges against Columbus, yet took this opportunity to strip him of his monopoly. The savvy navigator had initially made a deal securing sole enterprise of all voyages to the New World. This had always irritated the rapacious king, yet with the current turmoil, this gave the Crown some legal elbowroom. Columbus would be allowed to return, but he no longer held a seafaring monopoly. Furthermore, a full fleet of ships would even proceed to the New World before Columbus, with some men being covert operatives.

Adding further to Columbus' misery was King Ferdinand's top advisor, Bishop Fonseca, who proved to be even more intolerant and devious in his plotting to destroy Columbus. Harboring a strong prejudice against Columbus and Italians, Fonseca had previously purloined the financial bid for Columbus' second voyage to gain firm control, almost bankrupting the Italian banker Gianotto Berardi. The bishop had also sent Alonso de Hojeda to the New World to undermine Columbus.

Meanwhile, in May of 1499, Francisco de Bobadilla was appointed governor of Hispaniola while Columbus was detained in Spain. However, after Bobadilla's inept and cruel, yearlong reign, he was replaced by another devious Spaniard, Nicolás de Ovando. The atrocities grew.

Columbus' honor was tarnished by his dismissal, his lands in the New World were stolen, but at least the Crown had dropped the charges and he could explore the Caribbean once again. This had always been his ultimate quest, and this now brings us to his last voyage.

Columbus' Fourth & Final Voyage

Upon leaving the Spanish port—on May 9, 1502—Columbus immediately headed westward to find that elusive passageway. To his credit, Columbus actually made landfall on current day Martinique and then found the exact spot where the future Panama Canal would link both oceans. It was a relatively narrow section of land, but to Columbus, it looked like Asia or perhaps just another large island.

The natives he encountered told of another huge body of water just across the landmass, but it was a nine-day hike. Columbus was not thrilled with the idea of his seafaring crew hiking through the dense, bug-infested forest, and he had good reasons not to. The intense heat, thick jungles, and mosquito-swarming swamps were notorious for inflicting illness (although they had no idea what malaria was), and the earlier unexplained deaths of many of his men clearly must have aided his decision. Furthermore, Columbus was seeking a water route to India not another land route. Therefore, logic dictated that this huge body of water could be easily reached by sailing around the obstruction; so the admiral weighed anchor and set sail once again.

Traveling along the coast, the crews and their ships were bedeviled by the scorching tropical sun. To their dismay, the ships began taking on water. Shipworms had latched onto the fleet's hulls and were gnawing their way through the soggy timber. The watery parasites eventually sank the small fleet near the shore, as Columbus desperately ran his ship aground on the beautiful but uncharted island of modern-day Jamaica.

With his half-eaten ship beached, Columbus was further burdened by a severe decline in health. Wracked by gout, arthritis, and other debilitating ailments, Columbus was confined to minimal activity, and worse yet, with an irritable and restless crew. Sailors only knew how to busy themselves with daily chores upon the rolling seas, so idle time on land became a major quandary, especially for an ailing admiral.

It wasn't long, however, before the castaways encountered natives. Although they were a primitive race, they fortunately appeared friendly. Columbus quickly established a rapport with the natives, bartering various beads and trinkets for food. This vital exchange went on almost daily. Here again, the digests clearly reflect how Columbus approached each new encounter; namely, by open signs of friendship and making every effort not to incite or threaten them; however, if they attacked, a firm response would follow. Nevertheless, as uninvited guests, Columbus ordered his men to return to the beached ship routinely at nightfall and log in for good measure.

Again, many primary sources indicate how Columbus interacted with the natives, and they clearly dispel ruthless hostility. On Columbus' third voyage, he had encountered natives that curiously rowed out toward his ships. He ordered his crew to wave and invite them to come closer. After some failed attempts, Columbus said:

"I had a tambourine brought up to the poop and played, and made some of the young men dance, imagining that the Indians would draw closer to see the festivities. On observing the music and dancing, however, they dropped their oars, picked up their bows, and strung them. Each one seized his shield and they began to shoot arrows at us. I immediately stopped the music and ordered crossbows to be fired."

Here we clearly see how the natives initiated hostilities. However, there is the slight possibility that the natives mistook the friendly gesture of dancing to music as a war dance. That both peoples were not familiar with each other's traditions also added a deadly dynamic. Therefore, unfortunate calamities arose from both parties, as either hostile actions or misunderstandings, and modern revisionists should not be too quick to assume that the white man was always the one in error.

Nevertheless, weeks passed on the strange island, and Columbus' crew grew increasingly unnerved, and rightfully so, for it was clear that they were dreadfully marooned. The sailors' ships had served as their propelling legs and now they were frightfully crippled. Columbus knew their situation was desperate, as the odds of a Spanish caravel passing their uncharted isle were astronomical. But although Columbus was physically ill, his mind was never idle, for the admiral had indeed devised a plan.

Columbus discreetly summoned his courageous crewmember, Diego Mendez, and secretly relayed the plan. Secrecy was necessary to avoid ruffling the egos of his crew, as he knew that none would volunteer. The plan was for Diego to set sail on a small native canoe in search of Hispaniola by using Columbus' astute coordinates. There were no illusions, the perilous rescue mission, even if successful, was beleaguered by the fact that Columbus' adversarial replacement, Governor Ovando, now ruled in Hispaniola. Furthermore, Ovando had already made his position well known—Columbus was banned from returning to the island. But every sailor knew that the nautical rules of distress must prevail; after all, they were all fellow seamen loyal to the Spanish Crown.

As expected, when Columbus openly presented this daring plan to the crew, they quickly exchanged glances, then peered back at their commander with blank stares. The crew knew the plan was a death sentence; however, as planned, Diego Mendez boldly stepped forward and volunteered, while only Bartoloméo Fieschi followed. Outfitted with only three days of food rations, Diego, Fieschi, and six natives climbed aboard two log-hollowed canoes, and set sail into the choppy Caribbean Sea.

Meanwhile, the island's natives started to grow more impatient with their white-skinned guests, who now appeared more like well-settled gatecrashers. To Columbus' dismay, many stressful months passed without word. There was no way of knowing if Diego drowned, made landfall on Hispaniola, or even got stranded on another island.

During Diego's disquieting absence, Columbus' crew grew even more restless and divided. Half had conspired secretly and broke out in open mutiny. Taking arms and wreaking havoc, the mutineers faced an equal band of loyalists, but failed to prevail. Angrily, they fled, heading deep into the heart of the island. During their rampage, they prodded the natives to kill Columbus, and also demanded food and raped their women. Worse still, the mutineers began killing the natives who didn't comply with their demands, thus provoking a direct reprisal. This forced the brutal mutineers to retreat and regroup.

Columbus and his loyal crew, who remained defenseless on the open beach, were further endangered. Worse yet, Columbus was running out of items to barter for food, and the natives were growing more impatient and hostile. With Columbus' resources and his clever peace negotiations failing fast, the shipwrecked crew had to respond fast or face certain annihilation.

Columbus was painfully aware that he was not only outnumbered but ill equipped militarily. All that remained between life and death was his intellect. As the greatest navigator in his time, Columbus was fortunately well read in the sciences. This naturally included astronomy, for Columbus had even advanced the art of navigating by the stars. Knowing that a lunar eclipse was scheduled to occur in the next three days, Columbus hatched a brilliant scheme.

Setting his plan in motion, Columbus summoned a meeting with the natives. As the suspicious tribesmen gathered around, he assertively proclaimed that his God was superior to their lunar idol. He then ceremoniously hailed himself as his God's personal messenger. As the natives nervously listened, Columbus demanded their full obedience, or they would insult his mighty God and reap his deadly wrath. As a demonstration of his omnipotence, Columbus confidently declared that his God would blacken their cherished lunar orb in three days hence.

The fateful evening finally arrived, and the natives' eyes were anxiously fixed upon the night sky. Suddenly they were horrified by a diabolical spectacle—for right before their eyes their all-powerful lunar disc was indeed blotted out of the sky! Filled with fear, mixed with humble praise, the natives repented. Columbus peacefully stood his ground and assured them that his laudable God would restore the moon if they continued to bring food. Delighted with the reprieve, the natives eagerly complied. Due to Columbus' astronomical knowledge and astronomical wit, he was able to turn the tables without bloodshed, and in so doing, managed to save the lives of his entire crew.

Meanwhile, braving the restless seas on his weather-beaten canoe, Diego finally spotted land. To his amazement, he found Hispaniola exactly where Columbus had plotted. Once again, Columbus' keen knowledge saved the day. As the tiny canoe made landfall, Diego ran to the governor and summoned for help. To his astonishment, Ovando flatly refused immediate assistance, and instead, showered him with lame excuses.

Interestingly enough, the shady governor was racking up a bloody record of barbarism on the island, yet ironically this did not make waves. Being appointed by Bishop Fonseca, Governor Ovando did not have many worries, nor did he have any desire to rescue Columbus. In fact, both he and the bishop would be delighted to see the troublesome Italian fade into oblivion. As for Columbus' Spanish/Italian hybrid crew, they, too, were expendable. Most shockingly, Columbus and his crew were to remain shipwrecked for over a year.

Diego tried everything possible to gain favor and secure a vessel, but to no avail. Diego's appalling story quickly spread, however, and did not sit well with the residents of Hispaniola, some of whom still admired Columbus. Even those who were mistreated under his administration knew this was outright murder. Under growing pressure by the Hispaniolans, and fear of the Queen receiving word of his gross negligence, Governor Ovando was forced to make a move. His grand gesture was to send a single caravel. But the scheming governor only ordered the ship to locate the island, deliver food, and naturally quench his devious curiosity—was Columbus even still alive?

The caravel set sail and followed Diego's reverse coordinates. Slicing through the uncharted waters, the obedient captain duly spotted the island. Locating Columbus and his crew, the captain requested permission to board the beached vessel. The admiral invited the captain into his rotting cabin, while the castaways buoyantly cheered outside. As the captain ducked and entered the moldy hull, he immediately informed Columbus that Diego Mendez was alive, and then handed him a letter from his loyal crewmember.

Columbus began reading Diego's note, while the captain nervously imparted the Governor's bad news. Columbus abruptly stopped reading as his eyes lifted from the paper to fixate on the messenger. As the captain uneasily finished relaying his orders, the admiral sprung to his feet in disbelief. Columbus was momentarily speechless: there would be no rescue!? The captain meekly added that he was only instructed to drop off some wine and pork. Columbus exploded! The captain recoiled and frantically tried to reassure the infuriated admiral that Diego Mendez would very likely be making a rescue voyage in the near future. His lame words, however, couldn't quench the fire.

As the captain anxiously exited the cabin, his eyes inadvertently met those of the stranded castaways. Quickly, he turned about, and made a beeline to his ship. Columbus' crew stood momentarily dumbfounded.

As the ship raised anchor and began to set sail, the crew likewise exploded. Running and surrounding the beached ship, they vehemently cursed Columbus for his rivalry with Governor Ovando, as that—in their minds—caused their predicament. Even some of the loyal crewmembers threatened mutiny. Columbus stood firm; pacifying them with the news that Diego was still alive and would come soon. Hence, any revolt would be severely punished under Spanish law. The crew backed down.

Back in Hispaniola, Diego's laborious task reached fruition. He had finally managed to purchase a ship on Columbus' sterling reputation and good credit, which had always remained intact among seamen. Quickly setting sail, Diego made his way back to the dreadful island.

As Diego's ship came into view, the stranded castaways couldn't believe their eyes. When their fellow shipmate landed ashore, they turned toward their admiral with huge grins, saddled with remorseful eyes. They had blamed their commander for being stranded for over a year and facing almost certain death, yet Columbus had ensured their survival. They could finally leave the godforsaken island, with all its pain, death, and sin, far behind.

Despite Columbus' obsession, which often drove his crew to the limits of human endurance, the admiral managed to survive the trials and tribulations of a seemingly orderless and merciless world by using his sharp intellect and sheer determination.

Bitterness, however, filled Columbus' heart. He was unable to fulfill his life-long quest, was stripped of his discoveries by a greedy king and devious bishop, and left for dead along with his entire crew by a soulless colleague who refused a mandatory rescue mission and personally stole his dominion. Unfortunately, this ultimate insult added to his already withering health, and the tired admiral only sought the solitude of home. Upon his return to Spain, Columbus refused to even lay eyes upon the contemptible king or his foul bishop. Avoiding the limelight that once beamed over him, Columbus sank into obscurity.

This final and gloomy chapter of a spectacular man and colossal achievement is a sad and tragic ending for a man who had been a life-long servant of God (albeit colored by the dogma of his time) and a loyal subject to his king and queen.

Beyond the shipwrecks, hurricanes, mutinies, reprimands, demotion, insults, thefts, and near-fatal abandonment, Columbus also had to look forward to his great name being practically forgotten during his last years on earth, and quite deplorably, completely forgotten for over two centuries thereafter.

Worse still, after his death, Columbus' name would be passed over and another explorer's would be used to name the New World's two huge continents. His sacrifices and suffering, like those of many famous Christians, was for a monumental cause, and for that the Western world owes Columbus its eternal debt and gratitude.

Columbus 400th Anniversary Stamp issued during the
1893 Columbian Exposition in Chicago.

AMERIGO VESPUCCI:
Continental Car Salesman

The world was changing drastically during and especially after Columbus' eventful life; cartographers could not keep pace with the windfall of new discoveries and the world map's ever-changing form. Portugal was Spain's ultimate rival, and with its superior naval fleet, they eventually managed to discover the eastern route to India. This was due to Vasco da Gama, and his new course of sailing south around Africa's Cape of Good Hope in 1497. Additionally, the Portuguese had previously signed a treaty with Spain, claiming dominion over large portions of the unexplored seas.

Nevertheless, King Ferdinand, with the aid of his cunning companion, Bishop Fonseca, wanted nothing more than to curb Portugal's expansion. Most importantly, they wanted to prevent the Portuguese from learning about or pilfering Spain's treasure trove of new discoveries, which Spain in turn had wrested from Columbus. Therefore, the bishop contacted the reigning pope, who also happened to be of Spanish descent, with a request and an offer. The request was to aid the kingdom of Spain. However, the alluring offer was for the Vatican to expand their Christian kingdom into a New World. The pope, who eagerly took the bait, was none other than the infamous Borgia barracuda, Pope Alexander VI.

Pope Alexander promptly drafted a series of devious papal bulls. Amid the sanctimonious rhetoric, Alexander devised an imaginary demarcation line, which ran north to south in the Atlantic Ocean and just west of Portugal's Cape Verde Islands. To the loss of all others, all points west of that line, which constituted the Atlantic Ocean and all unknown territories beyond the visible horizon, would belong to Spain and, in a religious sense, the Vatican.

With the firm alliance of Spain and the Vatican blatantly sealed, Portugal and other nations seemed unwilling to intervene, especially since they viewed these newly discovered islands as wastelands inhabited by primitive natives. This gave Spain a significant lead in discovering more lands in the New World, while completely stripping Columbus of his lands, dreams, tribute, and wealth. Unfortunately, another disappointment awaited Columbus.

As early as 1499, a fellow Italian explorer followed Columbus' route, and with far less talent garnered even greater acclaim, or at least his name would. Amerigo Vespucci was born in Florence and actually lived in the house next door to the famous artist Sandro Botticelli.

After working in a lackluster string of menial and even unsavory professions, Amerigo found employment in the Medici's service, but soon relocated to Seville, Spain. While there, he eventually became associated with Gianotto Berardi, an Italian banker who, upon envisioning Christopher Columbus as the golden goose, devoted all his time and financial resources to the courageous navigator.

After losing the bid to finance the second voyage (only receiving a small portion of the journey to outfit, since Bishop Fonseca opted to power-manage the fleet), Berardi fell ill and subsequently died.

Being his primary beneficiary, Vespucci was left to manage Berardi's affairs. With Columbus falling out of favor with the Spanish monarchs and amassing hefty debts, the magnificent golden goose had instead become a malignant white elephant. Vespucci needed to cut his losses and move on to another profession. Being Columbus' major outfitter, Amerigo naturally heard many of the famous navigator's amazing stories firsthand. Furthermore, although Columbus had initially failed to procure financial rewards during his early explorations, he did inform the king, and Amerigo, about the abundant pearl fisheries he had located off the shores of what today is Venezuela. This was a compelling lure—one that seemed to promise Ferdinand a stellar fortune and Vespucci worldwide fame.

Without training or experience for any position aboard a caravel, Vespucci secured passage to the New World with one of Columbus' former mates turned-captain. At that point in time, several new independent expeditions were sponsored before the king even allowed Columbus to set sail again, as this was during King Ferdinand's policy of stripping Columbus of what he called a monopoly. As Columbus' star faded even his revelations of potential windfalls were stolen when Vespucci's ship sailed directly toward the pearl fisheries.

The new captains of these fleets all understood the importance of securing something financially tangible, since future sponsorship, as well as personal wealth, rested upon tangible results. In a phrase, the New World was open game.

One of Vespucci's former jobs was as a jeweler; hence his selection as a crewmember seems to have been initially granted for this reason. Vespucci wasted no time, however, in gaining recognition, not to mention the titles of pilot and astronomer. Much of this was due to Vespucci's aggressive drive for success and even stardom. This habitually involved the use of pretense and self-promotion, and successfully led to his securing a second voyage in 1501.

Vespucci's second journey took him along the shores of South America, and allegedly south of the equator, where he made many observations about the natives and the exotic flora and fauna. He also seized the opportunity to conjure up fallacious astronomical claims, which included having a secret mastery of the astrolabe. Amerigo also drew his own maps in addition to his romantic and illusory notes. Many of his observations, however, have recently been noted as being almost direct quotes of those made previously by his hero, Christopher Columbus. Nevertheless, Vespucci had come to realize that the huge land mass was not Asia, as Columbus assumed, but actually a new continent.

Upon his return, Amerigo wasted no time in professing to be an astrolabe expert and the most qualified cartographer of the New World. Selling himself as a scientist rather than a simple seafarer, Amerigo won the confidence of the royal court. During this time, Amerigo stayed at Columbus' house, picking the brain of the dejected but still brilliant master.

Their relationship was nothing short of odd, for while Amerigo deeply admired the admiral, and even won his confidence as a fervent supporter, it seems his own burning desire for glory and recognition led to a series of events that undermined his friend and master even more. Whether this was intentional or out of his control has been debated, but it appears Amerigo's own hype and spin enthralled publishers who were likewise eager for fame and fortune, and thus started a chain reaction that quickly became uncontrollable and most unfortunate.

Nevertheless, armed with Columbus' astute input and his own experiences at sea, Amerigo's confidence and verve won him favor and high office. He not only managed to win a financial reimbursement for Columbus, but his new official role of Pilot Major entrusted him with establishing an academy in his own house. Here, Amerigo would train all of Spain's sea captains in the use of the astrolabe and be solely responsible for commissioning or declining their service to the Crown. Furthermore, Amerigo was assigned the task of compiling charts from all New World voyages to construct new and updated maps of the rapidly emerging western hemisphere.

Amerigo's observations of the New World were immediately published in a small book called *Mundus Novus*. It became a bestseller and quickly hurled Amerigo's name into the spotlight. Rapidly overshadowing even Columbus, Amerigo's name resounded in almost half of all the travel books being published at that time.

Adding weight to this momentum was a letter allegedly from Amerigo to Piero Soderini, who was a member of the Medici regime in Florence. The thrust of the letter laid claims to an impressive array of observations and discoveries. This mysterious document later became known as the Soderini Letter, which evidently was compiled by an anonymous author. The letter contained many fragments of observations by Vespucci that mirrored Columbus directly, as well as the bogus claims of landing first and making four voyages, none of which Amerigo could lay claim to. More importantly, however, Amerigo's maps were sent to his German friend, Hylacomylus in France, who happened to be a premiere publisher of maps. (Hylacomylus was a fanciful Greek pseudonym, as his original German surname was Waldseemüller.)

Even though Columbus had lost all favor and fell into almost total obscurity, Hylacomylus cautiously withheld publication until the ailing navigator was safely dead. Whether this was intentional or happenstance is not known, however, when Columbus died in 1507, Hylacomylus published Vespucci's maps. Hylacomylus' successful publication not only displayed the intriguing design of the New World but he allegedly took it upon himself to label both huge continents "America."

Either this was a genuine gesture to honor his friend Amerigo for the rights to print a spectacular map, or, more likely, was part of a prearranged agreement between mapmaker and publisher, where the mapmaker declined royalties in favor of eternal fame. Whatever the deal, the instant success and volatile ignition of sales quickly sparked other mapmakers to follow suit. Spreading like wildfire, even the Spanish monarchs could not suppress the hot news, as the New World would be forever branded with the fraudulent name of Amerigo rather than Columbus.

Vespucci Awakens America - Stradanus's engraving (1638)

For over two hundred years this error prevailed, and the world hailed Amerigo Vespucci as the discoverer of the Americas. Meanwhile, Columbus was marginalized to the point of being almost forgotten. It was only during the late eighteenth century that the true story of the Vespucci sham was revealed. Today some historians have reassessed Amerigo's complicity in this naming convention, and insist that it was largely instigated by Hylacomylus and then amplified by others in an unbridled chain reaction.

Serendipitous events have occurred throughout history, however Vespucci's successes did not seem to be the result of pure luck: his modus operandi consisted of weaseling his way into official positions of power without a proper resume, being in charge of mapmaking for King Ferdinand, and using his personal contact with Columbus to hone his own boastful claims. Between his ultimate authority in the map industry and his long established record of self-importance and being a glory hound, it seems evident that Amerigo had his hands in the inkwell for penning his name on not one but both colossal continents.

Nevertheless, the revelation of Amerigo's deceit had sparked the beginning of Columbus' long overdue rise out of the ashes of neglect, and, like a phoenix, he soared to the summit of his field and received universal acclaim.

Yet while the founding fathers of the United States and their generation were the first to catch wind of Columbus' disgraceful plight, the maps of the Western hemisphere had already been branded with Amerigo's name and irrevocably burnt into history. Vespucci and/or Hylacomylus had pulled off a monumental caper of global proportions.

For many Americans, it probably comes as a disappointment that two flawed characters, driven by the fortunes of fame and greed, hatched their continent's name. Yet beyond their dubious actions, the United States of America likewise had a long and checkered history in its rise to power. From its earliest settlers through the fight for independence and beyond, American history is filled with imperfections and bloody events. As such, it should come as no surprise that during America's founding, the Liberty Bell cracked and symbolically remains flawed. That symbol should offer a constant reminder of how the trail to grand and noble ideas is always flawed, for even though many believe America was constructed under divine guidance, it was essentially left to the fallible and even unsavory hands of mortal men and women to build.

Therefore, fantasies of a utopian founding should remain in the books of ancient history, such as Homer's attempt to recreate a glorious and purified past for Greece, or Virgil's attempt for Rome. In contrast, the recorded history of America's founding should remain true and sobering, in the sense that we must understand the unpleasant actions that were taken while also understanding human nature well enough to know that those actions were often necessary to arrive at where we are today. Amerigo's burning need to better himself drove him to take risks based on his personal motives, but it also added momentum to a new exploratory development—one that needed a proactive spokesman or propane salesman to keep the flame burning. In a sense, Amerigo had innate American traits, for the world never saw a greater PR man, advertising wizard, or Continental car salesman than Amerigo Vespucci.

Too often history has shown that even great discoveries or ideas can lapse into obscurity, and although the New World was exotic and exciting, sponsorship was the only way to continue the quest. Therefore, salesmanship in portraying the New World as being more than just beautiful islands, inhabited with primitive natives and pretty flora, was mandatory to encourage investors as well as adventurous souls willing to risk life and limb. Amerigo, more than anyone else, sparked the intense media hype being generated at the time, and that was crucial to the cause, despite his being undeserving of the high acclaim and honor his name would garner.

Columbus' pioneering courage, and Spain's egregious attempt to strip him of his rightful discoveries, rank, and possessions, was somewhat mirrored by our brave fledgling nation and its fight against imperial Britain, which likewise tried to oppress and strip the colonists of their rights. Although Columbus made mistakes, his intentions were noble and largely selfless, and his spirit was emboldened with an indelible drive that is nothing short of remarkable. In this crucial sense, it is quite fortunate that the future United States of America would inherit his bold and courageous spirit. Even though Columbus never had the opportunity or resources to regain his rightful land or title, the revelation of truth two centuries later did restore his honor.

Among all the ancient explorers who sailed the rolling seas, Columbus majestically rides the crest, which not only dwarfs his rivals but also eulogizes his courageous name and spirit. Unfortunately, unmerited claims have always been part of human nature and America's history was certainly not immune. Over the years, there has been a rising tide to discredit Columbus. The first signs appeared at the five-hundredth anniversary of Columbus' discovery. The politically correct apologists mounted a huge smear campaign that maligned the courageous navigator by raising suspicious accusations of his heavy-handed governorship of Hispaniola and his mistreatment of the natives.

Beside the fact that this unwanted position was thrust upon Columbus by King Ferdinand, who had ulterior motives, it's odd how Ferdinand and Governor Ovando literally got away with mass-murder, yet only Columbus was shackled and maligned, despite his documented plea of innocence and the evidence of foul play to discredit him. What we do know is that Ferdinand and Bishop Fonseca plotted to undermine Columbus, and they succeeded in stripping him of his possessions, with the added bonus of defaming him in the process.

Moreover, these critics have gone a malicious step further by denying Columbus his rightful entitlement of discovery. Their attack is based upon the fact that the Vikings had previously crossed the Atlantic and hence they discovered America first. Most are well acquainted with Leif Ericsson's discovery of Vinland, which is modern day Newfoundland, however, several key issues must be considered.

First, Columbus and Europeans had no knowledge of any previous discovery or Northern routes. Although the Vikings used the icy waterways along Iceland and Greenland to reach the island of Newfoundland, which the Vikings eventually abandoned, the most important fact is that they never publicized this discovery. Hence, it remained completely unknown to all others.

Second, the Vikings even deceptively named the landmass that was green and lush, Iceland, and the icy lands, Greenland. This was simply a selfish and ultimately vain attempt to deter followers. Although some modern scholars speculate that the so-called Little Ice Age caused Greenland to become icy and that the land was actually green when the Vikings, Eric the Red, and his Norsemen first landed, the fact remains that their refusal to share knowledge or intermix with the natives doomed their existence when the frigid icy weather did come.

The native people of these frigid landmasses had developed superior ivory spearheads with reverse jagged edges that efficiently killed fish. This enabled the natives to survive, while the Vikings' land-based animals (which they brought with them) died in the cold climate. The Vikings believed that they were superior to the natives, however, so they never bothered to adopt their hunting skills. This mistake, coupled with their isolationist mentality, caused their own demise. Therefore, in the final analysis, the Vikings' secret ventures remained just that, for their discovery died due to their own selfish mistakes, and for the rest of humanity they remained completely unknown and utterly useless.

In contrast, the explosive and international acclaim of Columbus' initial discovery, which was amplified by Vespucci, began the volatile chain reaction that opened up an entire hemisphere to a new era of exploration. Furthermore, this single action profoundly altered world history forever. For as Thomas Edison would say centuries later, "The value of an idea lies in the using of it." This was true of Gutenberg, who did not invent the printing press yet bequeathed it to the world, and it would be true of Columbus, who though not technically the one to land first, officially introduced the western hemisphere to the rest of the world.

As mentioned, word of Columbus' discovery spread so rapidly that soon after, exploration and trade routes were bustling with caravels sailing along Columbus' mid-Atlantic course. Like a portal to another dimension, Columbus bequeathed to the Old World the golden key to a glorious New World, a gift to humanity that defies calculation.

KING FERDINAND:
Calculating Conqueror

The great Spanish empire that emerged during the Renaissance came about due to the strategic marriage and territorial union of Isabella from Castile and Ferdinand from Aragon (Aragon being a significantly smaller region). Both rulers cared little for bookkeeping, and as such, it wasn't long before their budding empire was faced with dire fiscal problems.

Added to these dismal internal affairs were serious external dilemmas, such as the threat of Portugal's growing navy, and the recent conquest of Constantinople, which severed all trade routes east. As such, the funding of Columbus' bold expedition was aimed at replenishing their ill-managed vault and getting them out of the red.

Upon Columbus' miraculous discovery, Ferdinand lost no time in not only plotting to conquer the entire western hemisphere, with the aid of the equally corrupt Spanish pope, but also in eradicating Spain's internal woes as well. While Queen Isabella was said to have been superior in intellect to her husband, Ferdinand had a raw lust for power, which he gained by common street-savvy and deceit. Despite the ugliness of his motives, Ferdinand was extremely capable and ruthlessly effective. After stripping Columbus of his lands, rank, and honor, Ferdinand built a world-class navy, and he and his wife also became master helmsmen of the Spanish Inquisition, with the aid of their wily first mate, Bishop Fonseca.

Ferdinand and Fonseca appealed to their fellow Spaniard at the Vatican, Bishop Rodrigo Borgia (who later became Pope Alexander VI), to put pressure on Pope Sixtus IV to issue a papal bull that would endorse their inquisition. It was nothing more than religious cleansing to scour Spain's "tainted" populace with a Christian wire brush. Pope Sixtus may have silently appreciated the Muslim cleansing agenda, but he truly needed Ferdinand's military aid, so he allegedly conceded with reluctance.

Ferdinand then appointed the infamous Tomás de Torquemada, who directed the *auto-da-fé* "act of faith" campaign, which vigorously hunted and condemned Jews, Muslims, and atheists. Those under the Inquisition's Gestapo-like eye were forced to convert, while those who refused were tortured, executed, or forced to flee Spain.

These broad persecutions were the invention of an unholy trinity, with the Royal Crown and Bishop Fonseca being the ultimate architects and Torquemada being the fanatical head foreman and executioner. Meanwhile, the pope was a disheartened accomplice who sold his soul and the dignity of the Catholic Church in exchange for military defense.

Previously, Ferdinand had cleverly managed to broker a deal with the Vatican, whereby the pope granted Ferdinand power to appoint his own bishops in Spain. From his position of power, Ferdinand also prohibited the pope from passing a bull without first getting his royal consent. The French monarchy had managed to do the same, which was the reason Spain and France never revolted against the Roman Catholic Church. Meanwhile, Germany and England never managed to broker such deals with the Vatican, and as a result this further motivated Germany's feisty monk, Martin Luther, to establish his own Lutheran sect, as well as England's King Henry VIII to depose the Catholic Church in favor of his own English Protestant sect.

King Ferdinand was a scheming tactician who knew how to use valuable connections to achieve ultimate control. Recently, some theologians have lauded one of Ferdinand's rare and benevolent gestures when he passed laws in favor of treating the American natives with kindness. This gesture, however, warrants scrutiny. First, this good deed was prompted by Father Montesinos who had witnessed the oppression firsthand, and as such brought it to Ferdinand's attention. But when Ferdinand's actions are compared to Father Montesinos', it becomes clear that only the good Father deserved being called benevolent.

Second, and most importantly, King Ferdinand was locked in an alliance with the pope; therefore, he had to make a visibly pious gesture or risk losing the Vatican's support. Despite his military superiority over the Vatican, Ferdinand faced other nation-states that posed a threat, so the Vatican, with its wealth and multinational congregation, was a crucial ally.

Most revealing of all is that Ferdinand did little to nothing to enforce these laws, which further validates his lack of concern in this regard, for his sights were set upon replenishing his depleted coffers and world conquest. In this capacity, Ferdinand did rather well.

The Spanish empire grew as the heirs of Ferdinand and Isabella carried it forward, yet it was doomed to failure from its very inception. The sprawling empire, which has impressed many, was actually like a glittering matador adulated by the masses. Standing proudly with his huge distracting red cape, the crowd was unaware that the powerful engine actually running the show was the foreign beast. Once the flamboyant matador squandered his funds, he could no longer afford another powerful beast. That is when the grand spectacle ended and it became clear that the essence of the show was, in fact, bull. Bull, in that it was a hollow empire sporting a dazzling façade, and bull, in that the real engine that made the empire run was the foreign bull market.

To clarify this fanciful analogy, this amazing empire rested solely upon foreign imports, for Spain did not have adequate terrain or resources, besides sheep for wool. Therefore, Spain relied upon foreign eatables, clothing, textiles, loans from Italian bankers, Italian-made cannons and weaponry—it even imported warships along with their international crews. In effect, all the major necessities for maintaining an empire came from outside sources.

Spain even exported whatever raw materials it had, only to re-import them as finished goods. The Spaniards were, in large measure, consumers only. Therefore, the gold and silver that Spain reaped from its New World settlements were turned into coinage that once again left Spanish soil to buy imported goods. Thus only a fanciful aura of glittering magnificence was created, which was precariously based upon negative cash flow. (This lazy approach of outsourcing and relying on other nations for manufacturing goods brought about the eventual demise of the Spanish empire and serves as a warning to the American empire today.)

Hence, Ferdinand and Isabella founded the Spanish empire, which although impressively exerting immense influence worldwide, ran itself into debt. Their kingdom was bequeathed to their grandson, Charles V, who in turn sought huge loans, totaling some 29 million ducats. Charles was an able leader and through royal family inheritance, war, and intrigue managed to expand the Spanish empire. Charles—like his grandfather, Ferdinand—inaugurated another brutal inquisition when the Reformation threatened to overtake the Netherlands. The matador king slaughtered over 100,000 fellow Christians for simply being tagged as Protestant, which to Charles meant heretic. When his son Philip II inherited the throne, along with the royal family's chronic debt, the younger matador was only able to keep the grand red cape flowing for one year. That is when the bull market died, and the Spanish empire collapsed.

Ferdinand's great name has long been remembered in history due to his powerful partnership with his wife, Isabella, both of whom are credited with uniting Spain, and more importantly, establishing the first global empire, spanning two hemispheres. However, the latter was only made possible by Columbus' incessant prodding and courageous discovery.

Moreover, it can no longer be ignored that Ferdinand was one of the principle architects of the Inquisition, the power hungry king who, while frantic to refill his empty coffers due to poor management, allowed many of his minions to wreak havoc in the New World, and was the deceitful schemer who robbed Columbus of his just rewards and even temporarily besmirched his great name. As such, the dirty truths of Ferdinand's crimes were like oil in water, and have risen to the top.

THE BORGIAS: *The Pernicious Pope and Devious Duke*

A swirling wind blew across the Tuscan hills, twisting the towering cypress trees like a manic Van Gogh painting. In the midst of this gale stood Duke Cesare Borgia and his newly appointed military engineer, Leonardo da Vinci.

Leonardo was highly recommended to Cesare by many who had witnessed his magnificent works of art, mastery of mathematical perspective, and seemingly infinite array of interests. They had also informed Cesare of da Vinci's secret obsession with engineering and science, coupled with an impressive gift for invention.

Cesare's military successes were like a magnet that drew talent, and money was no object. Being the illegitimate son of the immensely powerful Pope Alexander VI, Cesare had few financial worries and could easily compensate his personnel.

Wearing his flamboyant black beret with a white plume, the Duke haughtily approached Leonardo, as his military entourage marched close behind.

"So, Leonardo, I am told you can perform miracles, not only with oils, but with engineering and math, as well."

"Duca, everything in nature is composed of mathematical elements."

Cesare smiled. "Yes, like the number of cities I conquer, the rivals I kill, or the amount of taxes I collect!"

Cesare's soldiers looked at their leader with pride as they released a hearty barrage of sinister cackles.

"No! Not human nature," Leonardo replied. "Nature itself."

A silence quickly befell Cesare and his men as they all simultaneously turned toward Leonardo.

"Go on, *continui,*" Cesare commanded.

"Duca, I have studied Aristotle, and conversed with many of our greatest mathematical minds at the University of Padua. However, most important, are my own studies that have revealed many truths about nature. Its immense and complex construction, at its most minuscule level, is actually built upon elements of mathematical proportions. I have yet to figure out those equations, but they all fit together in various combinations forming an infinite variety of wondrous matter, which our eyes perceive daily. Yet, most are blind to these glorious doorways to knowledge. Instead, they rely upon the speculation, and oft-repeated verbiage of others, without looking or experimenting for themselves. *Ignoranza,* I tell you, the world is plagued with ignorance!"

Cesare's men looked at one another, unsure of how to react, until one bellowed, "What the hell did he just say?"

Igniting a guffaw, the garrison sounded like a wild bunch of donkeys, until Cesare blasted, "You damn idiots, *silenzio!* He obviously speaks of you!"

Lowering their heads, like scolded dogs, the soldiers stood, uneasy and even more baffled. As Cesare turned to address Leonardo, one of the soldiers spotted a man on horseback in the distance. The unmarked rider was heading their way and now began charging up the hill.

"Cesare, someone approaches!" the soldier exclaimed.

Instinctively, the armored watchdogs all wielded their swords as all heads turned toward the intruder.

Cesare turned, and barked, "He rides alone, stand down!"

Breaking into a leaping stride, the horse chewed up grass and gravel with his hooves as he made his way up the steep hillside. The muscular Spanish mustang feverishly approached, then stopped tersely, as his rider urgently tugged back on the reins.

Trying to steady his horse, the rider announced, "Pope Alexander VI has summoned the immediate presence of Duca Cesare Borgia."

One of the soldiers boldly approached the rider and growled, "This better be an official summons."

"It is, sir, it is!"

Upon receiving the document the soldier carefully inspected the scroll's wax papal seal. He knew that the pope's *pescatorio*, or Fisherman's Ring, doubled as a signet ring that left a unique impression in the sealing wax. Looking back at Cesare, the soldier nodded, confirming its authenticity.

Cesare smiled. "Yes, I know he's official."

The soldier squinted. "But how? He wears no official colors. Do you know him, my Lord?"

Cesare grinned and shook his head. "No, no, I could tell by the horse he's riding. The mustang is my father's favorite from the old country."

Cesare then cocked his head, gazing over at da Vinci. "My father beckons me, Leonardo, so I must depart. But as I had previously informed you, it is imperative that you survey this entire region and render precise maps. They are crucial to our plotting future campaigns. Terrain plays an important role in military strategy. Something many fools ignore. So precision, Leonardo, is paramount."

"You need not worry, *il mio* Duca. In addition to supplying you with the best maps your eyes shall ever see, I shall also show you designs for military weapons and fortifications no mind has ever envisioned or thought imaginable."

Cesare smiled. "From the impressive recommendations by my compatriots, I trust you will indeed surprise and please me, Leonardo. Be well, and don't hesitate to ask for anything you may need in fulfilling your task." Cesare then leaned over and whispered, "Even if it means muzzles for these buffoons!"

Leonardo laughed, and then thanked his new patron. The headstrong leader swiftly mounted his horse, and with a terse tug, quickly swiveled about. Designating two of his men as escorts, Cesare then motioned to the messenger to take the lead. With their spurs pricking their horses' loins, the quartet briskly departed for Rome.

The restless, evening sky grew even darker as gloomy, purple clouds choked the last remnants of cobalt out of the atmosphere. Thunder rumbled in the distance as veins of lightning ripped through the heavens. Riding up toward the recently built Sistine Chapel, erected previously by Pope Sixtus IV, the messenger pointed to the chapel's door. "That is where the pope wishes to meet you. He commanded that you go alone."

Cesare motioned for his men to stay put as his eyes surveyed the area. Slowly, he dismounted his horse and tethered it to a post. As Cesare cautiously advanced, a bolt of lightning suddenly illuminated the structure. Cesare looked up, his upper lip twisting as he released a subtle grunt. The chapel's mundane façade did not impress. Continuing forward, Cesare finally reached the arched doorway.

As the howling winds ravaged the trees, Cesare pushed open the door and entered the dark chapel. Taking only two steps, he then used his back to close the wind-blown door, keeping his eyes glued to the dark and silent interior before him. He was soon struck by the pungent scent of the two fragranced candles, some twenty feet away—their tiny flickering flames struggling to illuminate even the smallest sections of the vast chamber. Gazing up at the unadorned plaster walls and high vaulted ceiling, Cesare was overwhelmed by a macabre sense of being ensnared in a vacant tomb. Cautiously, Cesare took small halfhearted steps when suddenly a faint metallic sound irritated his eardrum.

Cesare soon realized that the culprit was a squeaky set of door hinges, emanating from the far side of the chamber. As his eyes squinted to focus, a dark rotund figure appeared in the doorway. Flanking the huge silhouette were two slim figures, each bearing an oil lamp.

Astutely aware of deadly coups, Cesare slowly placed his right hand over his sword's pearl-inlaid handle. As the three figures approached, their footsteps icily reverberated throughout the empty chamber. Cesare vigilantly glanced to the left, then right, his keen peripheral vision even managing to scan his back. Slowly, the obscure silhouettes began to emerge from the darkness.

Then the familiar voice of his father finally signaled, "Is that you, my son?"

With a sigh of relief, Cesare replied, "Yes, father, it is I…Cesare." With a smile, he calmly lowered his sweaty hand and wiped it on his trousers.

The pope, majestically adorned in a bejeweled vestment, at last appeared. His broad face, lit by the flickering lamps below, produced a sinister effect that at first startled Cesare.

Then the pope smiled and extended his hand, revealing the golden *pescatorio*. Cesare respectfully lowered his head and kissed his father's ring.

"It has been far too long, Cesare."

"Yes, father, it has, but indeed we're both busy men, and share the same responsibilities."

The pope's two clergymen recoiled with offense as one intrusively lifted his lamp to illuminate Cesare's face. In a voice reeking with consternation, he declared, "Young man, you are addressing the pope! How dare you compare your actions to his Eminence? Show some respect!"

Sensing Cesare's blood about to boil, Alexander quickly interjected, "Please, my son is a very spirited stallion. We are in private quarters and his words here are spoken not to a pope, but to his father."

"Your Eminence, with all due respect, we are fully aware of Cesare's lineage, but we must also advise you, as is our duty, that such practices spawn repetition and, as such, will repeat themselves in public. It is blasphemous for Cesare to think his station equals yours. He must learn obedience. After all, Your Holiness, you are our Lord's most exalted here on earth, you are the vicar and overseer of the Holy See."

Before Alexander could reply, Cesare exploded, "You mangy little flea! You best *wholly see* this!" Cesare unexpectedly snuffed the clergyman's candle out with his two bare fingers, and continued, "Beware of my powers, priest. Your pious words may control the delusional masses, but certainly not me. For I know very well the truth of our existence, and you're both just charlatans! Remember this, we are all made of flesh and blood...for if I were to slit your throats, blood would surely flow, not the symbolic wine or wrath of your ancient God. You see, my little vermin, it's just that I, like my father, have the balls to seize opportunity in this earthly domain. That his rule falls under the banner of

God, and mine under a coat of arms makes absolutely no difference, no difference at all! *Capisca?!"*

As the other clergyman attempted to squeak out a reply, Cesare quickly plunged his deadly index finger into his chest. "And the ones who should learn obedience are the insignificant fleas like you! Who at their best can only survive by clinging onto their all-powerful host. So, let me shatter your fragile delusion, both of you. It is leaders like *us* who rule this domain. So, shut up and enjoy the ride!"

Alexander finally took action. "Cesare, *basta!* Your temper has always been like Vesuvius. It will reap the same deadly results one day if you don't learn to harness it. And, my son, despite the madness that reigns here on earth, I firmly believe in our Lord Jesus Christ. So, for the sake of our heavenly Father and your earthly father, please, show some respect."

"Father, you know I will not tolerate being reprimanded by feeble little insects. If I offended you, father, forgive me. But as for them…to hell with them! I have killed real men for less, men sheathed in rigid bronze armor and wielding razor-sharp daggers, not feeble little fairies like this, who flutter about in flimsy cassocks. Perhaps we should speak alone, man-to-man, without these damn pesky fleas hovering about and whining in my ear."

Alexander's face turned red. "Cesare, I now command you…*basta!* (Enough!) And that, my son, comes from no feeble little flea! For your life's blood, in body and estate, is very much under my influence." Glancing at his two escorts, he added, "And as for you two, perhaps it is best you leave us. I have many important things to discuss with Cesare, and we have all wasted precious time."

Seething in silence, the two clergymen made an about-face and proceeded toward the exit. Disgusted by Cesare's lack of respect and the pope's tainted lifestyle, their minds began reeling in humiliation.

They each saw this whole debacle as the fruition of Alexander's many transgressions, which they were forced to bear in silence. Sure they enjoyed the power and prestige of being the pope's aides, but they couldn't stomach the entourage, which in private they chided as the Barbaric Borgia Brigade. They loathed being constantly reminded and incensed by Alexander's power politics and shameful indiscretions. The pope made no attempt to conceal his many children, and he flagrantly flaunted his many love affairs. Such as his latest scandal, where he had the portrait of his mistress made to look like the Virgin Mary, then mounted it over his bedchamber's door.

In desperation, one of the clergymen's eyes rolled upward as he silently prayed, *Dear Lord, please end this sacrilegious nightmare!*

As they passed through the chapel's exit, they eagerly slammed the door behind them without even turning their heads. Continuing their forward trajectory, they tenaciously kept their backs to what they knew was a repugnant mess.

Secluded in the dark chapel, Alexander lit a wall-mounted candle and slowly turned back toward his son. "Cesare, you know I have always done my best to make up for the lost time I could never spend with you as a boy."

Cesare nodded as his father continued, "I have consistently supported your efforts, and I do so because I have full faith in your abilities. Likewise, you have repeatedly shown that my investment, financially and affectionately, was sound. So I never wish to see outbursts like that again when you're on papal grounds."

"Very well, father, but then don't summon me here anymore. Let's meet on neutral ground from here forward."

"Cesare, you really are a stubborn bastard!"

"Indeed I am, Papa, on both accounts!"

Father and son burst out laughing and warmly embraced. Their acknowledging smiles confirmed that the spoiled apple indeed doesn't fall far from the rotten tree.

Alexander then stepped back as his paternal smile vanished. "My son, I have some very critical tasks that I can only entrust to you. Two of my bishops have conveniently passed away. Long story short, they were nosey pains in the ass, but I need you to secure all their possessions and properties."

Cesare looked at his father with a sinister smile. "Has father done something naughty?"

Alexander rolled his eyes. "No, no, the old farts died naturally. Listen! Obviously, this must be executed in a most discrete fashion. I need you to sell off their estates to friends or close associates of ours so as not to arouse the clergy or congregation's suspicions. Try to secure a maximum price, as those proceeds, my son, will help fund your campaigns in the Romagna."

A devious grin etched Cesare's face. "Consider it done."

"But Cesare, please understand the broader picture here. Almost two hundred years ago, Pope Clement V moved the papacy to France, where it lasted for a hundred years. Over that time, Rome lost control over much of its people and territory," as Alexander continued, his face reddened with rage, "that is intolerable and will not stand! Moreover, let us not forget how King Charles of France made his advances to remove me, or should I say *us* Borgias, just a few years ago. Fortunately, his concern over the reaction of the people thwarted his efforts, for we were never so close to losing our heads. So, we must take this very seriously."

As dutiful son nodded, doting father continued, "However, I have been making some headway with King Ferdinand of Spain, and we might be able to gain a sizeable foothold on some new and possibly fertile territories across the Atlantic Ocean as well."

Cesare's covetous eyes widened. "Holy shit! That's fantastic!"

Alexander shook his head. "Must you continue to act like a horse's ass in God's house?"

Cesare shrugged his shoulders, but then his eyebrows suddenly lifted. "Speaking of horses and Ferdinand, I hear the king has that Columbus fellow shipping your favorite Spanish mustangs over to the new world."

Alexander nodded. "Yes, it's a great animal. I'm sure it will come in handy over there."

"Indeed, I absolutely love them. They outrun the best of the rest and have great stamina. I see you outfitted your messenger with one."

Alexander nodded. "Yes, and I can also see why you like them, because they're a bit like you—wild!"

Father and son grinned, yet Alexander's face quickly regained gravity. "Never mind the mustangs, Cesare, remember, we must regain control of these wayward city-states all around us. They have deplorably abandoned the one and true papacy here in Rome. You shall indeed govern over all these provinces, Cesare, but they must be reunited with their true nation state and religious obligations. Rome must not lose its iron grip. Rome's survival, and more importantly, our family's survival depend on it!"

The two tightly embraced, then started to walk toward the chapel's exit. As their footsteps echoed in the cavernous chamber, Cesare peered about. "You know, father, I hate to bring up horses again, but this chapel looks like a stable. Someday you should have it decorated, perhaps with a nice fresco. It's really rather cold and depressing in here."

The pope smiled. "Yes, perhaps you're right, my son." Alexander gazed up at the cracked and bumpy masonry as they approached the exit. "After all, an illusionary fresco would nicely conceal the ugly rock underneath."

❋   ❋   ❋

As time would tell, the avaricious Borgias did nothing to decorate the Sistine Chapel; that would occur under Pope Julius II when he commissioned Michelangelo to decorate the ceiling, thus turning a vacant, cold chamber into a glowing masterpiece. However, despite the magnificence of the illusionary fresco, it could never truly hide the ugly rock underneath—namely the reprehensible deeds of ignoble popes like Alexander and his Borgia brigade who brought shame upon sacred ground—for truth always bleeds through camouflage, eventually.

LEONARDO: *Intellect Amongst Ignorance*

In the flourishing city of Florence, a hot humid breeze swirled over the banks of the Arno and down its narrow streets. Traversing the cobblestones was a rich assortment of industrious souls, all busily trying to make their mark, earn a gold florin, or buy a favor.

En route to the Palazzo Vecchio, Leonardo da Vinci walked briskly past the Baptistery, barely gazing at Ghiberti's famous bronze doors. Normally, Leonardo would have paused to analyze the magnificent bas-reliefs, but the master had been recently appointed, and now summoned, to a special committee. Their task: to determine the optimal location of a new colossal statue by a young, dynamic talent named Michelangelo. The statue in question was called *David*.

The young sculptor had managed to salvage a discarded monolith of white marble that was deemed flawed and unusable by a fellow artisan. By using it, Michelangelo not only triumphed over a physical roadblock, but also sculpted a shocking new masterpiece that won the attention of his talent-infested city. Having been accustomed to the petite and lean bronze *Davids* by Donatello and Verrocchio, Florence was stunned by Michelangelo's muscular gargantuan that stood almost 14 feet tall. This spectacular *David*, who even towered over Goliath, was ideally proportioned with pronounced and precise anatomy, save for his over-sized hands, which intentionally evoked David's raw strength.

Many Florentines attempted to attribute these powerful hands to Michelangelo's subliminal intention of projecting the power of Florence, however, they were almost certainly fashioned to project the indomitable power of the statue's dynamic creator. For Michelangelo had previously stunned all by boldly carving his name across Mother Mary's blouse in his *Pieta*. The proud youth had heard rumors that some were attributing his work to another sculptor, an unimaginable affront. Consequently, Michelangelo signed his masterwork, and in such a blatant fashion that the entire world would never doubt who was its creator.

However, Michelangelo's *David* did also mirror the spirit of Florence, for both the statue and the city stood fearless, proud, and determined—to the rest of the world, they radiated invincible power. Therefore this significant icon required strategic placement, and who better to be on the committee to make such a vital decision than the man many Florentines hailed as the greatest savant of the age. However, just as art is subjective, so too is the human mind when assessing the capabilities of others, as ingrained proclivities, snobbery, and even jealousy are traits that affect such decisions, for what appears as a luminous diamond to one person is considered cheap glass to another.

Leonardo fixed the brim of his hat, blocking the blistering sun, as he strolled past the Baptistery. Seeking the comfort of shade, he brushed his right hand along the building's cool pink and white marble walls. Then touching his forehead, Leonardo managed to cool his cranial engine by several degrees.

Out of the corner of his perceptive eye, Leonardo spotted two well-dressed men—one, very tall and thin, the other, short, broad and barrel-chested. As they plowed through the crowds, the two men abruptly changed course and headed directly toward Leonardo. Each man strut with his head held high, as the thin man bellowed commandingly, "Leonardo! *Un minuto, arresto!*"

With that, the two men formed a roadblock. Leonardo apprehensively stopped, as the thin man tenaciously continued, "It has been rumored that you have engaged in the high art of philosophy. Moreover, I hear this is without ever having learned to speak Greek." Straightening out his stiff collar, he continued, "That happens to be my area of expertise, Leonardo, and it would be most wise of you to allow me to critique your work."

No sooner had he spoken, did the hefty man add, "And it has come to my attention, Leonardo, that you brazenly claim to have invented new castle designs and weaponry that surpass anything ever devised." With a sinister cackle, he added, "I must say, to me it sounds like flagrant poppycock, and from a man who has not so much as attended one day of formal schooling for that matter."

Leonardo's fleetingly perplexed expression turned sour. "*Signori*, first of all, you have rudely forced your acquaintance without so much as an introduction. Second, I do not make it a habit of discussing my philosophies or experimental endeavors with interlopers. So, just who are you?"

The thin man's face wrinkled with contempt. "I assumed you recognized us; after all, we are both professors at the university, and leading citizens of Florence. I am Professor Bastone and my colleague here is Professor Barilotto. Let me assure you, I am the leading expert on Plato and Aristotle, and I, better than anyone, can correct all the flaws in your treatise."

Leonardo smiled as he took a step back and eyed the two men from head to toe. "*Signore* Bastone, I can clearly see your expertise and agenda. It is to criticize and demean the worth of others in an effort to enhance and inflate your own. However, I must warn you, my fresh and invigorating philosophy runs counter to some of the stale air that stagnates in your university's moldy chambers."

Bastone's head recoiled with disdain, as Leonardo continued, "Although I highly applaud the university, there are those who pompously reside in that book-clad world of academia who are saddled with idle minds, and they simply soil its good name. You may mock my lack of institutional schooling, but I propose to you that an academic man who only reiterates the words and deeds of others, as though of his own invention, is merely a parrot excelling in the mindless art of plagiarism. It is, in essence, a motionless mind, devoid of stimulation, a dark dungeon, devoid of luminance. In addition to dusty old books, *Signore* Bastone, one must delve into nature and scrutinize all its elaborate and mystifying details, and only then draw one's own conclusions. The words and wit of the ancients should only be used as a guide or supplement; for not all that was written is pure gold. Much tinsel abounds, and only a truly kinetic mind can decipher betwixt the two."

Bastone's bushy brows had flared skyward as sweat now rolled down his thin and angrily contorted face.

Barilotto looked at Bastone, and then sharply turned toward Leonardo with piercing eyes.

Before either could fire a retort, however, Leonardo continued, "And as for you, *Signore* Barilotto, yes, you are right about one thing. My castle designs do not follow the norm to which you so blindly subscribe. Yours makes a practice of adding miniscule and useless alterations to existing designs in a lame attempt to be praised novel. It is this lack of imagination or fear of change that cripples the mind, as well as progress itself. I prefer to analyze all the forces exerted on a particular structure, whether by nature or man, and then find solutions based upon investigative diligence and geometric experimentation. My models and calculations clearly support my unique visions, which you now call *brazen poppycock*."

The blood vessels in Barilotto's meaty face bulged, as he barked, "*Signore* da Vinci, I am privy to the confidence of many people of high esteem. The fact remains that I have not only heard of your plans, but have seen your confounded cartoon with my own eyes. A castle, since you never had the good fortune to learn in an academy, is intended to be a huge and intimidating structure to thwart even the thought of breach. This is based upon the careful study of the frailties of human nature, as well as architectural planning. Your plan is ludicrously squat, circular, and has smooth rounded walls, rather than being tall, square, and majestically detailed. Your series of rounded walls look like a group of concentric rings placed on the ground. It is simply mindless. It defies the norm for the sake of defiance. It aspires just to be different. And, that is the only thing you truly are *Signore* da Vinci, *different!* You're a round orb in a square-pegged world. Like that lunatic sailor from Genoa, you probably think the earth is round, as well. All you are is a pathetic dreamer, standing at odds against the entire world, which wisely knows better. You're just an illegitimate fool, with a shadowy pedigree!"

Bastone slapped Barilotto on the back, proud of his friend's erudite and personal attack, as the two men burst into a hardy guffaw. Bastone wheezed while Barilotto hooted.

Unexpectedly, Leonardo smiled and leaned forward. "Ah, but I know *your* pedigrees. What we have here are two heckling hyenas." Leaning back, Leonardo added, "I certainly don't expect creatures of your variety to understand the workings of the human mind, let alone mine."

Having won the attention and silence of the two predators, Leonardo crossed his arms, as Barilotto belched indignantly, "Oh, and what pray tell do you know that we do not?"

Leonardo placed his hands on his hips and leaned forward. "If either of you paused to realize that cannon balls would ricochet off these smooth rounded walls, as opposed to flat towering targets with nooks and crannies that collect rather than deflect, you might understand the lucidity of my designs. Consider this; those concentric rings are like an archer's target. They provide several tiers of reinforcement, all with the primary purpose of protecting and securing the command center in the middle, or bull's eye, which undoubtedly puts my design right on target. And as for my ballistics or revolving machine guns and armored vehicles, they would certainly go way over your four-legged heads. So, go ahead, indulge your arrogance and call me a dreamer, for it is only through such dreams that true invention and progress occurs."

Barilotto laughed bitterly. "Huh ha! Dreams have no place in our university. Our library's rich collection boasts the greatest texts by the brightest minds in history. And they're preserved and reserved for deserving minds only.

We are the entrusted elite who must protect and pass on the light of knowledge, while unfortunately residing among a throng of dim-witted dreamers like you. Your kind is correctly relegated to that subculture that resides left of center, where only whimsy and unproven claims abound. But alas, I suppose we must understand this, for it is certainly due to your lack of proper schooling."

Leonardo perceptively shook his head. "I see some at the university have become overtly cynical, and swift to dismiss dreams or unorthodox approaches to the art of inquiry. Well, I assure you, it is vital that the imagination be cultivated. It is essential to realize that the vast wealth of history's greatest thinkers, philosophers, architects, musicians, artists, scientists, political leaders, and religious icons had little or no schooling whatsoever. And even the humble Messiah himself, Jesus Christ, had no schooling. So what precedent did He bring to bear?"

A pensive look washed over both men's faces, as Leonardo continued, "Yet, there have also been many who have received the best education possible and yielded little or nothing in return. Consider how Nero was educated by Rome's foremost intellectual, Seneca, only to become a madman, or how Alexander the Great was tutored by Aristotle, only to remain a murderous general. However, don't misunderstand me, I know many professors of high esteem who deserve that honor. They have risen to fame by using their own cognitive abilities in tandem with the university's fertile library. But I'm afraid you two are attempting to rise by the hot air of your own inflated breath. Yes, you may be privileged to reside at the university, but that honor alone does not bestow upon you wisdom or high esteem. That must be earned. Genius can only be obtained by actively utilizing knowledge, for dormant acquisition is useless. So, *Signori* Bastone and Barilotto, the name da Vinci is founded upon solid and tangible deeds, not hot odorous gas."

The two men stood aghast and smoldered in silence. Angrily they glanced at each other, then back at Leonardo, as he resolutely continued, "So you see, one only needs to peruse a list of seminal doers of history—Euclid, Plato, Aristotle, Caesar, Augustus, Agrippa, Constantine, Dante, Brunelleschi, Gutenberg. They were all dreamers. Not delusional dreamers, but *kinetic* dreamers."

Both men frowned and grumbled vehemently under their breath, as Leonardo calmly grasped their adjacent shoulders and pushed each man aside. Without a word, he continued his journey forward.

Bastone turned, and finally blasted, "You're nothing but a blustering fool! Go ahead, walk your lonely path, but know this—you can never rise to our level!"

Leonardo stopped, and pivoted about. "Inflated by the winds of your own delusion you may rise up to the clouds, but alas, true genius transcends even the stars."

Leonardo then turned and vanished into the bustling crowds of Florence.

❊ ❊ ❊

Even as a youth, Leonardo stood apart from his fellow brethren. As an illegitimate child, Leonardo wasn't allotted the benefits of the wealthy. As such, in lieu of attending school Leonardo was placed in the artistic workshop of Andrea del Verrocchio by his father. While many of his peers eventually left the workshop to begin their careers, Leonardo lingered behind, perhaps more content conducting research and fueling his imagination than seeking patrons and dealing with the mundane order of business.

Nevertheless, there were those who viewed Leonardo as a curiosity, as indicated in the preceding fictional scenario, as well as in the proceeding factual essay.

Leonardo's insatiable quest for knowledge had lured him into perhaps the broadest spectrum of inquiry ever ventured by a single mind. Even more astounding was that he excelled at the majority of those endeavors. Leonardo became a leading figure in anatomy, engineering, botany, optics, weaponry, flight, hydraulics, music, theater, and sculpture, and naturally, he was the ultimate master of drawing and painting.

The vast amount of notebooks left by Da Vinci, not to mention all those regrettably lost, are not only staggering in volume but also indicate a man obsessed with the creation of visionary ideas, even at the expense of failing to gain funding or having the opportunity to build them. That Leonardo was under the employ of the eras most prominent men, like Lorenzo de Medici, Cesare Borgia, Ludovico Sforza, Pope Leo X, and King Francis I, but often did not have his designs implemented or, worse yet, failed to deliver on his commissions, remains somewhat of a mystery.

Although Lorenzo de Medici and his relative, Pope Leo X, had little patience and were happy to see Leonardo take on a new patron, all these great leaders had a great deal of belief in, and admiration for, this eccentric genius. That they put up with his independence and even contractual neglect only indicates that they all realized his genius and perhaps just wished for an opportunity to see one more masterpiece materialize. His *Virgin of the Rocks, Portrait of Cecilia Gallerani,* colossal Sforza Equestrian Monument and of course *The Last Supper* were all proof of that. If not, they would be content just to witness the endless font of ideas, odd contraptions, or even beautiful sketches that would emanate out of his deeply complex and radiant mind.

With the benefit of hindsight, we now know that some of Da Vinci's sketches for machinery were most likely renderings of existing devices that had intrigued him. Other great engineers existed: particularly Brunelleschi, who, many years before Leonardo's birth, invented cranes, elevators, scaffolds, and other equipment that were left scattered about many years after he completed his many architectural wonders. However, those today that negatively fixate on these particular sketches by Leonardo as being mere copies have missed the far larger picture. First of all, these sketches provided Leonardo with workable solutions that acted like an engineer's study manual today. These schematics laid the groundwork for the many wholly unique and often mind-boggling inventions that Leonardo did devise, and these have no predecessors. Moreover, many of these inventions would only see the light of day many centuries later in the distant future.

So although some critics like to focus on Leonardo's impractical inventions, like his colossal crossbow, we can see that his notebooks were just that, personal drawing boards were the master could indulge his imagination to devise and revise, or even discard, as needed. We must also realize that Leonardo experimented with weapons that were deemed too radical and never built. One design was a horse-drawn device with a rotating gear mechanism. It spun four helicopter-like blades, each capable of being outfitted with spiked clubs or a series of metal balls that would have clearly destroyed anything in its path. We must also bear in mind that just because these mechanical devices were never built or implemented by his royal patrons does not mean they were all improbable or unrealistic. Moreover, Da Vinci designed several variations of a multi-barreled rifle or cannon and even a rotating "Gatling-type" machine gun, the latter predating Richard Gatling's Civil War machinegun by four hundred years.

As for why Leonardo's sound weapon designs didn't make it into production; first of all, bravery and gallantry on the battlefield was the order of the day, and machines to kill en masse must have been viewed with doubt and probably distaste. Even five centuries later, Adolf Hitler initially rejected the use of machine guns on the grounds that they were not honorable weapons. The ease of killing so many without a struggle was almost equated to cheating. However, the chivalrous bravado of hand-to-hand combat would indeed eventually give way to technological mass-slaughter. So has mankind really become more advanced or less chivalrous?

Secondly, those with less vision do not always embrace novel ideas. Case in point, after several successful test flights by the Wright brothers with their pioneering new flying machine, they solicited the United States War Department with plans to retrofit their new invention for military use. The military brass was not convinced of the plane's worthiness and they flatly rebuffed the inventors. Three years passed, as the Wright brothers feverishly tried to entice European countries to buy their new fangled invention. Only after prolonged and exhausting efforts did Teddy Roosevelt's administration buy into the idea.

Knowing the extremely curious and restless nature of Leonardo, it is not hard to see that he would never jeopardize or abandon his scientific research to become a full-time salesman, especially for the promotion of a single idea. His time and energy was far too precious and much better spent at his miraculous drawing board, where even he must have been amazed at some of the ideas that materialized in his perpetually sparkling and mysterious mind.

Moreover, Leonardo is unique in that he often abandoned projects, whether being more interested in the initial creative process than with the menial or tedious chore of execution; being piqued by another alluring endeavor; or producing concepts that baffled and then humiliated his ornery patrons. Nevertheless, this self-determining behavior was a first, as no other artisan ever had the audacity to defy their patrons as often, or in the ultimate manner, as did Leonardo. Even Michelangelo, who was twenty-three years younger and had an ego the size of his colossal *David*, may have petulantly moaned about, and detested, his assignment to paint the Sistine Chapel, yet he obediently gave in to his master, Pope Julius II.

Meanwhile, Leonardo moved among his patrons clearly as their equal—or, in reality, their superior. This drove some of them mad, especially the incompetent and greedy Pope Leo X, whom, upon commissioning Leonardo for a painting, was infuriated that the artist began by mixing varnish. He blasted, "This man will never do anything, for he starts by thinking about the end before the work is begun."

What Leo failed to comprehend is that Leonardo was not the run-of-the-mill artist; he was a scientist, inventor, engineer etc. Leonardo had not only introduced the art of oil painting in Italy, but he was also drawn to experimenting with various paint mediums, resins, and varnishes. He very likely was still seeking to find the ideal solution when Pope Leo hired him, for we know Leonardo experienced several debacles previously. We also know that all roads leading to success are littered with failures. One was with Leonardo's famous fresco, *The Last Supper*.

Duke Ludovico Sforza commissioned *The Last Supper* for the refectory in the Santa Maria delle Grazie church in Milan. It was intended to be a typical fresco; fresco being a rapid and laborious process of using a water-based paint in wet plaster. This procedure severely limited the time an artist could work with the paints before the plaster dried. Obviously having an aversion to working at someone else's prescribed pace or even a mixture's hasty pace—in tandem with being a relentless innovator—Leonardo set out to devise a new methodology.

Da Vinci formulated a new resin and gesso mixture as a base, which sealed the wall and was allowed to dry. He then used either oil or tempera paint and worked at his own leisurely pace. Spectators noticed how some days Leonardo would enter the refectory and pick up his brush to make a small change to a minor detail and then leave. Other days, he would sit and just stare at the painting for great lengths of time and then leave, only to return the next day and work like the possessed from dawn till dusk.

However, the Dominican friars were getting annoyed at Leonardo's slow progress and they appealed to the duke, who pressured Leonardo to finish the work. The final result, however, was spectacular. The new process allowed Leonardo the time and ability to create fine detail and dazzling colors that were unattainable via the fresco method. The vision was simply breathtaking. Naturally his flawless use of perspective, which not only placed Jesus at the focal point but also made the scene look as if an extension of the dinning hall—along with his unsurpassed ability at drawing the human form—added to the awe. Instantly hailed by many as the ultimate masterpiece, Da Vinci's eternal fame was secure.

However, Leonardo's paint was not secure. His new technique to replace the time-tested fresco process had sadly turned into a dismal failure. Leonardo was destined to watch his glorious masterpiece slowly deteriorate, as the paint blistered and began to flake off bit by bit. By the seventeenth century, the sacred figures were mere ghosts of their former selves. Mindless restorations followed, whereby destroying Leonardo's sublime masterpiece forever.

Nevertheless, Leonardo had previously established himself as the most advanced, unconventional, and often-flawless artist of his day. Only a few years previously in 1483, Leonardo had painted the *Virgin of the Rocks*, which exemplified his unrivalled skills. First, Leonardo's composition, like the majority of his works, perfectly suited the subject and the theme that he wished to portray. The work exhibited a perfect state of balance that carried the spectator's eyes in the circular direction that he intended. While other artists often placed figures without rhyme or reason, Leonardo set the standard for strategically arranging many figures, as well as a single pose. Even a hand gesture or facial nuance was well calculated to achieve the desired result, i.e. the *Mona Lisa.*

Second, his pioneering use of *chiaroscuro*—bathing his subjects in light and shadow—was based upon his keen, scientific observational skills, which no other artist had ever exhibited. Finally, Leonardo's ability to draw and paint figures of anatomical correctness and express an inner human or even spiritual aura, when called for, were clearly talents that even Michelangelo or Raphael found difficult to rival.

Leonardo's intense technical studies of the human form—being the world's first anatomical illustrator to make diagrams of internal organs, arteries, veins, muscles and bones—clearly equipped him with the firsthand knowledge of how to draw and paint the human figure in any position and with complete accuracy. And although Michelangelo became his close rival, the sculptor often painted or even chiseled figures—particularly women—as if over endowed with bulging muscles. Barring Michelangelo's early works, which were more natural, his later works all exhibited both men and women of herculean stature. In fact, Leonardo even quipped about artists of his day drawing figures as if bags filled with rocks. One look at Michelangelo's rendition of *Eve in the Garden of Eden* or his sculpture of a woman representing *Night,* on his tomb for Giuliano de Medici, clearly demonstrates his obsession with masculinity and muscles. Softness and tenderness had sadly faded from his works.

Meanwhile, although only being a charcoal sketch, the womanly grace and spiritual transcendence found in the faces and bodies of Leonardo's *Virgin and Child with St. Anne and John the Baptist* display talents that no other Renaissance artist fully obtained, thus explaining why Filippino Lippi, when petitioned to paint this scene, declined, stating that it should be awarded to Leonardo instead, being that he was "a greater artist."

The HERCULEAN ART of Michelangelo
The Enigmatic Realism of Leonardo
Leonardo's Virgin and St. Anne and Mona Lisa display his soft realism as compared to Michelangelo's obsession with Herculean masculinity, as his painting of Eve and statue of Night (at bottom) both indicate.

Raphael's *School of Athens:* Raphael studied Leonardo's work and here displays his mastery of form and perspective. He honored Leonardo by using his likeness for Plato (center left) who is speaking with Aristotle. He used Michelangelo's likeness for Heraclitus (gloomily sitting in the foreground).

Leonardo was viewed as the great old master, even being honored by the younger (and heavily influenced) artist Raphael in his masterful work *The School of Athens*. In this grand fresco, which decorated the Apostolic Palace in the Vatican, Raphael used Leonardo's likeness to represent the wise old philosopher Plato, who, along with Aristotle, rightfully stood at the painting's focal point. Meanwhile, a sea of other great thinkers surrounded the two titans.

While many today may have expected Michelangelo to represent Aristotle, being the younger titanic force, Raphael instead used Michelangelo to depict Heraclitus, who was known as "the weeping philosopher." Raphael placed Heraclitus in the foreground sitting on the floor in a contemplative position, bearing a somewhat disturbed mood. This was surely due to Michelangelo's utter contempt for being forced to paint the ceiling of the Sistine Chapel, which he happened to be working on at the very same time.

Several years earlier, Leonardo had been appointed to a committee in Florence that was entrusted with determining the optimal location of a new colossal statue by the young and dynamic talent, Michelangelo. The statue in question was Michelangelo's *David*.

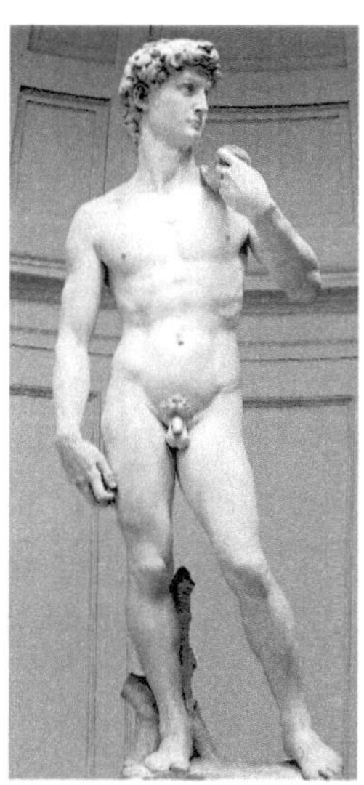

However, both Michelangelo and Leonardo would eventually leave Florence and find employment elsewhere, as the Renaissance was indeed a most turbulent era. And it was precisely these warring rivalries between city-states that forced dukes, princes, and even popes to seek and secure military engineers and architects. And this aptly brings us back to why these patrons eagerly sought Leonardo's multifaceted skill sets.

Ludovico Sforza of Milan and King Francis I of France proved to be Leonardo's staunchest patrons. They clearly recognized the protean genius before them and allowed Leonardo freedoms no other artist, scientist, engineer, architect, or festivities director ever enjoyed. Along with the many weapons Leonardo designed, we mustn't overlook his radical La Rocca Fortress, which he conceived for Duke Cesare Borgia. Here again, his drastic leap forward must have baffled his busy patron; however, Niccolo Machiavelli, the perceptive military thinker, had wisely approved.

The norm had been to construct towering monstrosities with flat angular walls and high turrets, which were meant to not only give the inhabitants a bird's eye view of the advancing enemy but was also intended to psychologically intimidate the invading foe. In essence, a fortress was intended to be a huge, menacing structure to thwart even the thought of breach.

Meanwhile, Leonardo devised a stealthy, low-profiled, circular building. It was essentially a series of circular rings with moats in-between. A larger moat surrounded the outer ring, while four rounded turrets sat outside the walls and evenly spaced. Appearing like a futuristic, streamlined complex, Da Vinci's La Rocca Fortress (or Ringed Fortress, as I call it) would have been able to fire upon intruders in any direction.

Most importantly, any artillery or cannon balls fired upon the fortress would have clearly ricocheted off its low and smoothly rounded walls. Meanwhile, underground tunnels conveniently connected all the rings to the central command tower. Leonardo's Ringed Fortress was a design that evidently didn't impress the ostentatious patrons of his day, but was clearly an amazing concept for a distant Star Wars age.

Interestingly enough, when the United States War Department decided that it needed a new headquarters building in 1941 they built the Pentagon. Although not circular, the design was a low profiled building consisting of several concentric rings.

Leonardo's prophetic and inventive genius has rightfully enamored millions. Many in his day (and many today) recognized Leonardo as being a polymath of the highest order. However, due to his illegitimate birth Leonardo never received a standard education, despite being fortunate enough to be accepted into Verrocchio's studio. This deficit caused some to mock him.

However, when we consider how many great thinkers, such as Thomas Edison or Henry Ford, also had no formal education, we must realize that a college diploma is not the sole means for judging talent or even brilliance.

In fact, as stated in the vignette, when we consider how Nero was educated by Rome's foremost intellectual, Seneca, only to become a madman, or how Alexander the Great was tutored by Aristotle, only to remain a warring general, we have to question just how important is education when we neglect the innate qualities of the individual being trained?

We know education benefits the majority, yet it's prudent to remember that many geniuses have forged their own paths, just as Steve Jobs and Bill Gates abandoned college to be two of this century's premiere star talents that changed the world. And Leonardo rightfully sits at the apex of human brilliance, along with his sagacious peers.

Bibliography
Primary list of sources.

A SHORT HISTORY OF BYZANTIUM – John Julius Norwich

AMERIGO – Felipe Fernandez-Armesto

ANCIENT GREECE: From Prehistoric to Hellenistic Times – Thomas R. Martin

ANCIENT ROME – Nigel Rodgers

ARE WE ROME? The Fall of an Empire and the Fate of America – Cullen Murphy

AUGUSTINE: A New Biography – James O'Donnell

AUGUSTUS: The Life of Rome's First Emperor – Anthony Everitt

AUGUSTUS CAESAR: Architect of Empire – Monroe Stearns

BERNAL DIAZ: The Conquest of New Spain, trans. J.M. Cohen

BEYOND BELIEF: The Secret Gospels of Thomas – Elaine Pagels

BRUNELLESCHI'S DOME – Ross King

CALIGULA: The Corruption of Power – Anthony A. Barr

CHRISTOPHER COLUMBUS: The Four Voyages – Translated by J.M. Cohen

CHRONICLE OF THE ROMAN EMPERORS – Chris Scarre

CHRONICLE OF THE ROMAN REPUBLIC – Philip Matyszak

CIVILIZATION: A New History of the Western World – Roger Osborne

COMPLETE WORKS OF TACITUS - trans. Alfred Church & William Brodribb

CONSTANTINE AND THE BISHOPS – H.A. Drake

CONSTANTINE'S SWORD – James Carroll

DANTE: The Poet, the Political Thinker, the Man – Barbara Reynolds

DIVINE COMEDY: Dante Alighieri, trans. John Ciardi

FORTUNE IS A RIVER – Roger D. Masters

GOD AGAINST GODS: The History of the War between Monotheism and Polytheism – Jonathan Kirsch

HADRIAN – Stewart Perowne

HOW THE CATHOLIC CHURCH BUILT WESTERN CIVILIZATION – Thomas E. Woods Jr.

KING JAMES version of the BIBLE

LOST CHRISTIANITIES: The Battles for Scripture and the Faiths
We Never Knew – Bart D. Ehrman

MEDICI MONEY – Tim Parks

MURDER AT GOLGOTHA: Revisiting the Most Famous Crime
Scene in History – Ian Wilson

NICCOLO MACHIAVELLI THE PRINCE AND OTHER
WRITINGS – Translated by Wayne A. Rebhorn

ROMAN REALITIES – Finley Hooper

SAILING FROM BYZANTIUM: How a Lost Empire Shaped the
World – Colin Wells

SAINT PETER – Michael Grant

SPARKS OF GENIUS – Robert and Michele Root-Bernstein

SPREZZATURA – Peter D'Epiro & Mary Desmond Pinkowish

THE ANNALS OF IMPERIAL ROME – Tacitus – Translated by
Michael Grant

THE ARCHAEOLOGY OF THE ROMAN ECONOMY – Kevin
Greene

THE CLOSING OF THE WESTERN MIND – Charles Freeman

THE DECLINE AND FALL OF THE ROMAN EMPIRE – Edward
Gibbon

THE FOURTH CRUSADE – Jonathan Phillips

THE GREEK ACHIEVEMENT – Charles Freeman

THE HISTORY OF ROME: Livy - trans. Valerie Warrior

THE LIFE & TIMES OF CONSTANTINE THE GREAT – D.G.
Kousoulas

THE LOST GOSPEL: Quest for the Gospel of Judas Iscariot –
Herbert Krosney

THE NAG HAMMADI LIBRARY: The definitive translation –
James Robinson

THE RENAISSANCE – Michel Pierre

THE ROMAN EMPERORS – Michael Grant

THE STORY OF THOUGHT – Bryan Magee

THE TWELVE CAESARS – Suetonius– Translated by Robert Graves

THE VICTORY OF REASON: How Christianity Led to Freedom,
Capitalism and Western Success - Rodney Stark

THE WARS OF THE JEWS – Flavius Josephus

WHY THE JEWS REJECTED JESUS– David Klinghoffer

WOMEN OF ANCIENT ROME – Don Nardo

The Author

Rich DiSilvio is an author of thrillers, mysteries, historical fiction and nonfiction. He has written books, historical articles, and commentaries for magazines and online resources. His passion for history, art, music, and architecture has yielded contributions in each discipline in his professional careers.

DiSilvio's work in the entertainment industry includes projects for historical documentaries, including James Cameron's *The Lost Tomb of Jesus, Killing Hitler, The War Zone* series, *Return to Kirkuk, Operation Valkyrie,* and cable TV shows and films such as *Tracey Ullman's State of the Union, Celebrity Mole, Blood Ties, Monty Python: Almost the Truth,* and many others.

He has written commentaries on the great composers (such as the top-rated Franz Liszt Site), and conceived and designed the Pantheon of Composers porcelain collection for the Metropolitan Opera, which also retailed throughout the USA and Europe.

His artwork and new media projects have graced the album covers and animated advertisements for numerous super-groups and celebrities, including, Pink Floyd, Yes, The Moody Blues, Cher, Madonna, Jay-Z, Willie Nelson, Miles Davis, the Rolling Stones, Alice Cooper, Queen, and many more.

As a software designer/developer, Rich pioneered the first interactive CD-ROM for educating staff and parents about Applied Behavioral Analysis (ABA) for training individuals with autism.

Rich lives in New York with his wife and has four children.

Other Books by Rich DiSilvio

Please visit your favorite online book retailer or library to discover other books by Rich DiSilvio, or sign up to receive special discounts at www.richdisilvio.com

My Nazi Nemesis (GOLD AWARD WINNER) is a fast-paced thriller that's razor sharp and unpredictable. Set between the horrors of Nazi Germany and Cold War tensions, the hunt for justice entangles Jack, Alois, Veronika, and Eleanor in a suspenseful tale that will keep readers guessing until its shocking conclusion.

A Blazing Gilded Age is the touching account of a poor coal-mining family's struggles and a searing look at the ugly underbelly of a golden era, one that transformed from an agrarian backwater into a world superpower. Featuring iconic figures, such as Theodore Roosevelt, J.P. Morgan, Mark Twain, Nikola Tesla, several presidents, and many others, *A Blazing Gilded Age* is a poignant saga destined to become an American classic.

Liszt's Dante Symphony: An unconventional thriller/mystery, replete with ciphers, spies, serial murders, and two intertwining tales that cover the rise of Hitler's Nazi Germany from its Prussian roots under Otto von Bismarck. It features, Liszt, Rossini, Ingres, Einstein, a string of composers, artists, scientists, and politicians, including Napoleon III and Adolf Hitler.

The Winds of Time is a robust, nonfictional tome that analyzes the key titans and main cultures that shaped Western civilization, while also debunking many of the myths and scribes that intentionally or mindlessly revised history, whereby misleading and distorting our understanding of history as well as our ability to truly learn from it. With America's future and very survival in mind, the author provides us with many lessons and warnings that only the past can provide.

YA children's books: ***Meet My Famous Friends*** and **Danny and the DreamWeaver**, the latter is penned under the pseudonym Mark Poe.

For updated info, visit DiSilvio's website above.

Special Note to the Reader

Thank you for reading *Tales of Titans Vol. I*

The short works presented herein were first conceived between 2005 and 2009, and released in the first Standard Edition of *The Winds of Time*, which featured a vast series of nonfictional biographies/studies and the quasi-fictional narrative vignettes. The vignettes, however, were later replaced with pure nonfictional content in the present Master Edition, which is still available.

For those interested in pure history and more info about these and numerous other titans of history, please consider reading *The Winds of Time*, a 740-page tome with a greater wealth of information. If you prefer historical thrillers about WWII and Hitler, please consider reading *My Nazi Nemesis* or *Liszt's Dante Symphony*. And for a searing look at America's past, please consider the historical novel *A Blazing Gilded Age*.

And if you're inclined to help a writer, please take a moment to post a brief review about this sampling of my work on your favorite retailer's website or social media forum.

Afterwards, send an email to info@dvbooks.net with the link to your review(s) and you'll receive **Special VIP Discounts** for my other books.

Thank you for your support!

Rich DiSilvio

M

N

O

P

Q

R

S

T

V

W